WORLD OUT OF STEP

Borgo Press Books by JOHN RUSSELL FEARN

*1,000-Year Voyage: A Science Fiction Novel * Anjani the Mighty: A Lost Race Novel* (Anjani #2) * *Black Maria, M.A.: A Classic Crime Novel* (Black Maria #1) * *A Case for Brutus Lloyd* * *The Crimson Rambler: A Crime Novel * Death in Silhouette* (Black Maria #5) * *Don't Touch Me: A Crime Novel * Dynasty of the Small: Classic Science Fiction Stories * The Empty Coffins: A Mystery of Horror * The Fourth Door: A Mystery Novel * From Afar: A Science Fiction Mystery * Fugitive of Time: A Classic Science Fiction Novel * The G-Bomb: A Science Fiction Novel * The Genial Dinosaur* (Herbert the Dinosaur #2) * *The Gold of Akada: A Jungle Adventure Novel* (Anjani #1) * *Here and Now: A Science Fiction Novel * Into the Unknown: A Science Fiction Tale * Last Conflict: Classic Science Fiction Stories * Legacy from Sirius: A Classic Science Fiction Novel * The Man from Hell: Classic Science Fiction Stories * The Man Who Was Not: A Crime Novel * Manton's World: A Classic Science Fiction Novel * Moon Magic: A Novel of Romance* (as Elizabeth Rutland) * *The Murdered Schoolgirl: A Classic Crime Novel* (Black Maria #2) * *One Remained Seated: A Classic Crime Novel* (Black Maria #3) * *One Way Out: A Crime Novel* (with Philip Harbottle) * *Pattern of Murder: A Classic Crime Novel * Reflected Glory: A Dr. Castle Classic Crime Novel * Robbery Without Violence: Two Science Fiction Crime Stories * Rule of the Brains: Classic Science Fiction Stories * Shattering Glass: A Crime Novel * The Silvered Cage: A Scientific Murder Mystery * Slaves of Ijax: A Science Fiction Novel * Something from Mercury: Classic Science Fiction Stories * The Space Warp: A Science Fiction Novel * A Thing of the Past* (Herbert the Dinosaur #1) * *Thy Arm Alone: A Classic Crime Novel* (Black Maria #4) * *The Time Trap: A Science Fiction Novel * Vision Sinister: A Scientific Detective Thriller * Voice of the Conqueror: A Classic Science Fiction Novel * What Happened to Hammond? A Scientific Mystery * Within That Room!: A Classic Crime Novel * World Without Chance*

THE GOLDEN AMAZON SAGA

1. *World Beneath Ice* * 2. *Lord of Atlantis* * 3. *Triangle of Power* * 4. *The Amethyst City* * 5. *Daughter of the Amazon* * 6. *Quorne Returns* * 7. *The Central Intelligence* * 8. *The Cosmic Crusaders* * 9. *Parasite Planet* * 10. *World Out of Step* * 11. *The Shadow People* * 12. *Kingpin Planet* * 13. *World in Reverse* * 14. *Dwellers in Darkness* * 15. *World in Duplicate* * 16. *Lords of Creation* * 17. *Duel with Colossus* * 18. *Standstill Planet* * 19. *Ghost World* * 20. *Earth Divided* * 21. *Chameleon Planet* (with Philip Harbottle)

WORLD OUT OF STEP

THE GOLDEN AMAZON SAGA, BOOK TEN

JOHN RUSSELL FEARN

Edited by Philip Harbottle

THE BORGO PRESS

MMXIII

WORLD OUT OF STEP

FIRST BORGO PRESS EDITION

Published by Wildside Press LLC

www.wildsidebooks.com

DEDICATION

For Eleanor Rose King

CONTENTS

THE GOLDEN AMAZON
by Philip Harbottle

In 1943 British writer John Russell Fearn decided to quit writing for the American pulp science fiction magazines, and to concentrate instead on books for the English market. Within a very few years he became established as a leading novelist in several genres, not only science fiction, but also mystery and detective fiction, and westerns.

His first new SF novel, *The Golden Amazon*, was published by World's Work in April 1944. In this story, a little girl of three years of age is made the subject of an idealistic scientist's illegal glandular experiments. The scientist's dream is to end world wars by creating a woman devoid of the usual lusts and frailties of mankind, who upon reaching maturity would institute a benign scientific rule. But the apparently successful experiment has a flaw: it instills into the girl a hatred for all men, and a ruthless cruelty. Her supernatural scientific gifts enable her to master atomic power, and practically leads her to destroy the world. She breaks the will and strength of men, and elevates women to positions of wealth and power. She also discovers human synthesis, and by this means she is able to escape retribution when she is eventually overthrown. She is seen to collapse and die, a victim of consuming ketabolism, echoing the memorable finale of Rider Haggard's *She*. In actuality, it was only her synthetic image, and this paved the way for the *Golden Amazon Returns*, and further sequels

Fearn sold reprint rights in the first novel to the prestigious Canadian magazine, the Toronto *Star Weekly*. The magazine carried a special Comics Supplement, the centre section of which was a 'complete novel', published in newspaper format. Aimed at a general readership, the novels were written by the top popular novelists of the day, including John Dickson Carr, Ellery Queen, and P. G. Wodehouse. They sold hundreds of thousands of copies, and the novels were syndicated to several American newspapers in the Maine and New York areas. The Amazon novels enjoyed extraordinary popularity (especially with Canadian housewives), and ran for the next sixteen years following the appearance of the first novel in the March 3, 1945 issue, ending with Fearn's sudden death in September 1960, aged only fifty-two. His final two Amazon novels appeared posthumously.

During Fearn's lifetime, only the first six novels were published in British hardcover editions from the World's Work in England, after appearing in the *Star Weekly*. This was because the publishers discontinued their entire fiction line in 1954. However, the Amazon novels continued to appear in the *Star Weekly*, eventually notching up twenty-four titles.

Fearn had resold paperback rights to the Canadian publisher Harlequin Books, but after publishing only the first three titles, they stopped publishing SF and other genre fiction to concentrate on their famous Romances line.

Meanwhile, as early as 1949, Fearn had realized that the Amazon series had the potential to run indefinitely. This presented him with a problem, however. The 'origin story' of the Golden Amazon was conceived and actually set during the Second World War. Subsequent novels were written during the war and the immediate postwar period, and projected their stories only a few decades into the future.

He very astutely realized that to keep ahead of reality, he needed to move the Amazon *further* into the future—first into the outer solar system, and thence to the stars. So with the seventh novel, he introduced a new main character, Abna of Atlantis—someone as equally intelligent, and even stronger than herself. These dynamics provided him with an *interstellar* canvas, thus ensuring that the series would remain ahead of reality.

Fearn's strategy was a great success, and the Amazon novels retained their popularity, ending only with his tragically early death in 1960. By then he had written a further twenty Amazon novels, and made preliminary notes for his next (which would later be written by Fearn's biographer, Philip Harbottle).

Long after Fearn's death, his entire Amazon series

would eventually see print from the pioneering US small press Gryphon Books in limited paperback editions, and later by the Canadian Battered Silicon Dispatch Box small press in their hardcover Omnibus series.

This new Borgo Press paperback series will be the first trade edition of all twenty-one of these later novels by Fearn, beginning with the seventh novel in the original series. First published in 1949 as *Conquest of the Amazon*, I have edited it slightly as *World Beneath Ice* (The Golden Amazon Saga, Book One) so that it can be read and enjoyed by new readers who may be totally unfamiliar with what had gone before. Subsequent novels have also been slightly edited for modern readers.

The publishers hope that this new series may create many more "fans of the Amazon." Meanwhile, any reader interested in seeking out the earlier six Golden Amazon novels will find that they are readily available on the internet, and in numerous earlier paperback and hardcover editions.

* * * * * * * * *

To date, readers can enjoy the following new Borgo Press editions:

Book One: *World Beneath Ice*

In destroying the threat of an alien invasion, the Golden Amazon had inadvertently caused a decline in the sun's heat, encasing Earth in an ice sheet that threatens to eliminate humanity. The Amazon encounters Abna, a descendant of Atlantis, stronger and even more scientifically advanced than she, and the ruler of an Atlantean colony still surviving in a protected environment on Jupiter. She refuses his offer of marriage, but agrees to form an alliance in order to restore the sun and save the Earth. One thing that Abna has not told the Amazon is that all the females of his race have been wiped out by a bacilli infection....

Book Two: *Lord of Atlantis*

A gigantic ridge of land rises from the Atlantic floor, causing massive tidal waves on either side of the ocean. Even stranger, both England and America are then assailed by an invasion of prehistoric monsters! A gigantic domed city rests on the newly risen plateau, whilst out in space an alien spacecraft orbits the Earth. Such are the mysteries and challenges facing the Golden Amazon, self-appointed governess of Earth, as she struggles to unravel the maze of mystery that was the deadly legacy of Atlantis!

Book Three: *Triangle of Power*

The marriage of Violet Ray Brant—better known as The Golden Amazon—and Abna of Atlantis should have ushered in an era of peace and scientific prosperity to the people of Earth. But an unexpected turn of events finds Abna betrayed and marooned on a satellite of Jupiter, and the Amazon flung far beyond the Solar System. With Earth's two protectors removed, the planet is now at the mercy of another Atlantean, the master scientist Sefner Quorne....

Book Four: *The Amethyst City*

The metaphysical union of the Amazon and Abna results in the mental creation of a fully mature daughter—Viona. Quorne, still struggling for domination, forces Viona into a marriage ceremony, and impregnates her. But with the intervention of Tarnec Brodix, a super-mind from an external universe, Quorne and Viona are separately flung into an ultra-dimensional limbo. Abna chooses to follow after his daughter, leaving the Amazon to brood over the disaster, alone in the Amethyst City of Saturn.

Book Five: *Daughter of the Amazon*

A miscalculation by the super-mathematician Tarnec Brodix destroys his universe, and the fault spreads into the Earth universe in the form of a Dark Tide of Absolute Nothingness. Unable to save himself, Brodix transfers his knowledge into the one mind powerful enough to receive it: that if Sefian, the son who has been born to Viona and Quorne. Sefian rapidly evolves, and, no longer human, after saving the Earth universe, vanishes into the greater universe, to seek new challenges. Then the Amazon is confronted with a further puzzle—a large section of the planet Neptune is discovered to be an exact duplicate of the Earth!

Book Six: *Quorne Returns*

The bacterial intelligences of Neptune plan to conquer Earth by replacing humans in key positions with alien duplicates. The Neptunians are themselves subjugated by the sinister Atlantean scientist, Sefner Quorne. Alerted to the threat, the Golden Amazon hits back by creating the ultimate doomsday weapon—only to precipitate a reprisal from the denizens of another universe....

Book Seven: *The Central Intelligence*

The Golden Amazon's arch-enemy, Sefner Quorne, discovers that all mental gifts, such as memory and creativity, are something that is broadcast throughout the universe by a Central Intelligence—and then interpreted according to the quality of the individual brain of the recipient. At the surprising suggestion of his wife, Viona, the Amazon's daughter, Quorne travels with her to the very center of the universe, in order to wrest the secrets of mentality from the very source itself!

Book Eight: *The Cosmic Crusaders*

The Golden Amazon renounces all ties with Earth when, together with her husband, Abna, and her daughter, Viona, she sets off on a journey to explore the cosmos. On the strange worlds of Alpha Centauri, she encounters Mizanu, the embodiment of evil—a planet-sized hypertrophied brain! Its baleful, crushing mental power threatens to reach out beyond the double-system of Alpha and Proxima Centauri to engulf the Earth and all the other inhabited planets of the galaxy—unless the Amazon can destroy it first!

Book Nine: *Parasite Planet*

The Cosmic Crusaders discover a fantastic world of mental parasites drawing form and substance from our own Earth, fifty light years distant. The planet is ruled by a being identical to the Golden Amazon herself— but an Amazon who's coldly scientific and vicious, mirroring the original Amazon as she had once been early in her career. Inevitably, they become locked in a deadly duel—to the death!

CHAPTER ONE
MYSTERY PLANET

So far from the world of Earth as to be beyond the reach of any scientific instruments, there drifted the *Ultra*, spaceship base and home of the Cosmic Crusaders.

At the moment the giant machine, created by the incredible minds of the Golden Amazon of Earth and Abna of Jupiter, was drifting in space at the center of the spawning flux of stardust unimaginatively named 'The Milky Way.'

When the Cosmic Crusaders had begun their mighty plan to spread science and peace amongst the stars, there had only been three of them—the Amazon, Abna her husband, and the copper-haired Viona, the product of their twin minds in fusion. But now there was one other, as mighty in physique and mentality as the original Crusaders—Mexone. Formerly an inhabitant of a planet now countless light-years away, the course of destiny had made him the husband of Viona, and that had automatically demanded that his physical and mental status be brought to the level of that of his wife and her parents.

So now the four Crusaders stood at the enormous bow window in the prow of the *Ultra* and surveyed. Surveyed as gods might, studying with an immeasurable indulgence the possibilities that lay before them.

"Do you suppose," Viona asked presently, her intense sapphire eyes surveying the deeps, "that there is anything more we can really do, father? Do you, mother?"

"Really do?" The Amazon turned in surprise—this graceful, majestic blonde with the muscles of forged steel. "But what a question! Of course there is!"

"Tired of wandering?" Abna inquired, with a dry smile.

"Of course not." Viona hesitated for a moment, and Mexone's powerful arm tightened about her waist. "It's just that— Well, we've seen so many worlds, and corrected so many badly-organized peoples, that it's hard to think of any more needing it."

Abna's smiling face became serious. "As long as there are living beings, Viona, there will always be difficulties and dissensions."

For some reason Viona did not appear to be listening. She was staring straight through the window into the star-draped canopy of space. Her eyes were bewildered, startled.

"Anything the matter?" the Amazon asked in surprise, catching her expression.

"I—I don't quite know." Viona did not take her gaze from space. Instead she moved lithely forward and pressed her face close to the heavily-insulated glass.

After a moment or two she turned her head quickly.

"I wasn't mistaken!" she exclaimed. "There's something queer out there! A sort of—of leap-frogging star, or planet!"

"A *what*?" Abna looked at her in amazement.

By this time Viona was being crowded by her father, mother, and Mexone. She indicated the star in question, separated from its nearest neighbors, and glowing with a faint ruby light.

"I may be wrong," Mexone said, "but I don't think it's a star at all. I believe I can just detect the outline of a disc, and if so, it is a planet."

"Star or planet, it jumped!" Viona declared flatly, and at that Abna turned aside.

"Soon find out what it is, anyhow," he said, and he crossed to the astronomical panel. In a matter of moments he had trained the telescopic equipment on the distant mystery, and the object loomed in view on the giant reflective screen.

A switch snapped under Mexone's fingers and darkness dropped. Now the unknown loomed clear and bright—beyond question a planet of vaguely Martian redness, a cloud or two floating in its clear atmosphere. The landscape itself was partly empty desert, but here and there were patchwork delineations that could have passed for cities.

Abna turned to the controls again and that which had been vague became clear. Definitely there were cities, apparently made up of curious, cone-like edifices, yet with roads which could have caused no surprise had they been on Earth.

"Planet, all right," the Amazon commented, pondering. "But the leap-frog business has me bothered. Just a moment while I check on its constitution."

The lights came up again, and for some minutes the Amazon was busy with the automatic analyzer. By its mathematical sifting of light-mass and other details, the instrument was able to determine every detail of the world in question without there being any need to actually visit it.

"Better have a close look at it," the Amazon decided, switching off the instruments. "Apparently there is no life that needs our assistance, but the mystery of the leap-frog technique more than intrigues me."

With that she went over to the main panel and started the *Ultra* forward from its drifting position. Within a matter of minutes the colossal machine was building speed upon speed, streaking over the two million miles of intervening space.

With scarcely a jar the *Ultra* came to a halt. The soft hum of the giant engines ceased. Abna led the way to the window and surveyed the exterior. In the immediate foreground was the reddish plain, which appeared to be natural rock—and about two miles away there lay the outskirts of the city. Seen here from ground level, the cone-like buildings looked surprisingly like an assembly of loom bobbins. Thus everything lay, in the torrid blue-white glare of the cloudless sun.

"I wonder," Abna said, with his teasing smile, "what would happen to us if this world suddenly decided to leap-frog now we are upon it?"

"All right, laugh!" Viona challenged crossly. "I tell you it did, and I also—"

"Look!" Mexone interrupted, pointing. "Life!"

It was not exactly that, but it was certainly something moving. It could have been a guided missile, or it could equally have had a guiding hand inside it. Whatever the answer, there now streaked across the sky in the far distance an object only classifiable as a space machine. It had none of the refinements or the enormous size of the *Ultra*, but at least it had maneuverability. It darted once across the city, clearly visible by the sun reflecting from its polished metalwork— then in a swiftly designed power dive it made a 'Z' in the sky and finally vanished from view somewhere to the rear of the city itself.

"Do you think we were seen?" Mexone asked, and after thinking about it for a moment or two, Abna shook his head.

"I hardly think so—that is, if there was anybody inside that machine. It could have been remote-controlled."

"Talking of remote control," the Amazon said, "we could see if they have radio...."

She switched on the apparatus, tuned it, and then stood listening in astonishment to the noises that came from the loudspeaker. Abna, Viona, and Mexone glanced at one another, wincing at the appalling cacophony bawling forth. It sounded exactly like an army of bad instrumentalists trying to play harps.

"What sort of a language is that?" Mexone demanded blankly, as the Amazon turned down the volume to bearable sound.

"No language at all," Viona decided. "Just plain, horrible noise!"

The Amazon switched off, and in the comforting silence the four looked at each other.

"Up to you, Viona," the Amazon said finally. "This is your particular pigeon. Do you think we should explore, or are the wastes of space more appealing? Remember, there may be danger here—danger of a type we can't envisage as yet."

"Nothing new about that, far as we're concerned," Viona responded, feeling that her courage was being challenged. "Yes, I think we ought to look around. How about you, Mex?"

"Whatever the Crusaders do, I do," he replied simply—and so it was decided.

CHAPTER TWO
WORLD OUT OF STEP

Ten minutes later, a test of the atmosphere having satisfied them that it was indeed breathable—as had been revealed in the earlier analysis from space—the quartet was on its way from the *Ultra*, having left the ship completely dead as far as any alien trying to start it up was concerned.

Walking on this unknown planet was both pleasant and exhilarating. The high oxygen content made breathing a deep and satisfying business, which in turn produced an energy never experienced on Earth, except perhaps in certain highly bracing coastal regions.

Abna was looking straight ahead, trying to form some kind of sense out of the cone-like buildings, but there seemed to be no satisfactory conclusion that he could reach. So finally they had come to the outermost edge of the quaint city and here they paused, each with a hand on their weapon belts, gazing down the main street with its queer buildings on either side.

"Houses or domiciles of some sort, I suppose?" Viona questioned at last, and the Amazon nodded.

"Presumably. But we—Life!" she broke off quickly.

There was no time to withdraw; not even time to dodge, as four inhabitants of this unknown world suddenly came in view from one of the buildings.

They were remarkable in appearance. The nearest resemblance the Amazon could think of was tulips, even to the color-scheme. The bodies were thin as pipe stems with truncated legs and rather broad feet. Shoulders, as such, did not exist. Instead there were enormous heads, as featureless and as glazed as tulip flowers. Arms seemed to be comprised of two tendrils of whip-like quickness at either side of the queer bodies.... There was no hint of clothing—so the general illusion of walking tulips that formed in the Amazon's agile mind was quite an apt one.

Then, as the Amazon and Abna were glancing at each other and wondering what to do next, more of the creatures came into sight, moving around, some of them discussing and others heading for different edifices. Though there did not appear to be many of the tulip people, the effect was similar to that of a gathering on any main street anywhere, except for the absence of vehicular traffic. And, at times, there floated to the travelers that impossible language which they had heard over the *Ultra*'s radio—though how it was produced when the creatures had no mouths was a mystery.

"Well, we can't stand here all day," Abna said finally, his hand still on his proton-gun. "Better go in the midst of them and see what happens."

He set the example by walking forward and the

Amazon came up immediately behind him. A little more reticently Viona and Mexone followed, until at length they had come into the midst of the nearest group of tulip people—and here at close quarters the real fantasy of the creatures became obvious. They were like something out of a dream—eight feet high, with their missing faces and enormous bobbing heads. But they were sentient and vital; there was no doubt of that.

Warily, the Amazon and Abna watched, Viona and Mexone behind them with their hands on their weapons. But apparently no hostility was intended for, when a few feet away, the tulip beings stopped and writhed their arm-like appendages in something that could have passed for a salute.

Immediately Abna took his cue and raised his own arm in solemn greeting.

"We salute you, friends," he said gravely, and inwardly wished he did not feel as though he were addressing a flowerbed. "We come from the deeps of space and would have audience with whoever is your ruler."

"Very well, that can be granted."

Abna blinked slightly. He was quite sure he had heard that response, and yet— He turned abruptly, and from the looks on the faces of his wife, daughter, and Mexone he knew it had been no illusion.

"They talk our language," Viona whispered in amazement. "And without mouths! This is certainly some planet!"

"Vibration," the Amazon said, as coldly practical as ever. "To say nothing of a high order of intelligence. They have absorbed our language in a matter of seconds—presumably by telepathic means."

"Your statement is correct, woman of space." It was impossible to judge which being was talking. "We are telepaths and have minds capable of both absorption and transmission of mental waves. Be assured that you are more than welcome here. If you will come with us, your wish to have audience with our ruler will be gratified."

Abna relaxed a little and took a hand from his weapon. He gave the Amazon a significant glance and then stepped forward, falling in behind the tulip being as he about-turned and went back up the street. To either side of them the gathered tulip people fell aside, which seemed to suggest that the leader was a high dignitary of some kind.

"Makes you wonder what we've got into," Abna murmured, as the Amazon fell into step beside him. "A planet that leap-frogs, populated by a form of life that's basically vegetable, and yet they are telepaths and have space travel."

"If they are telepaths we've got to watch ourselves," Viona put in. "They'll know all we're thinking about and planning before we can even say anything."

"There's a way around that, too," Abna told her. "Just blank your mind. I've trained you how to do it: now is the time to put it into practice."

By this time they had practically walked the length

of the street and followed their escorts into one of the larger cone-like edifices. Once inside it, with the eyes accustoming to the dimmer light following the brilliant sunshine, the full majestic beauty of the interior became apparent. The main hall they were now traversing appeared to be solid marble, the vaulted root supported in pseudo-Roman style by gigantic fluted pillars. In the midst of the marble ran traceries of deep yellow metal, which was probably gold.

"If you will wait," came the voice, "our ruler will be informed of your presence. We regret the appointments are not designed for your type of bodies, but that was something we could not foresee."

Their heads bobbing on their ridiculous bodies, the tulip beings departed and closed the door. In silence the travelers stared at the furniture. It seemed to be made up of curled creations, vaguely suggestive of an earthly helter-skelter on a small scale. Plainly the idea was that the tulip bodies could drape into the curved lineage as a human being sits in a chair.

"Well," Abna said finally, turning, "I shouldn't think even you, Viona, can be bored with this!"

"Bored! I'm fascinated! It's the most peculiar world we've yet come across—"

She paused and turned as the door opened into the room there came the two most remarkable beings yet. These were quite ten feet tall, and still conveying the same tulip-like effect as their fellows. One was a deep sea green with a huge and bobbing head—and the other a flaming, almost hurtful scarlet. They moved silently, like their fellows, pausing at length and both inclining their ridiculous, flower-like heads.

"Greetings," came a voice, of heavy bass. "This is an interesting occasion indeed, even though visitors from space are not unique. You, though, are very different from any we have yet encountered—and I note you are thinking the same about us."

"Yes," Abna agreed blandly. "We are. It would help if we knew which one of you is now addressing us."

The sea green one waggled his tendrils for identification.

"I am the ruler of this particular zone of the planet, my friends. Vashon by name. My companion here is my chief scientific adviser—Sazner."

Abna inclined his head. "Greetings to both of you. I am Abna of Jupiter. This is my wife—known as the Golden Amazon, of the planet Earth. Here is our daughter, Viona, and her husband, Mexone, of a world many light years from here."

"What do you seek here?" This time the voice was high and hard. It grated on the senses of the travelers, even though it was intensely distinct. Obviously it had come from the being who was scarlet.

"Nothing more than your friendship, and perhaps an exchange of information," the Amazon responded, staring at the blazing color of the creature and trying to weigh him. "We have traveled countless light years and were resting in space when we saw a queer thing— or at least my daughter did. This world of yours apparently jumped from one position in space to another and yet was not in the space between at any time."

Silence. In fact, more than silence. There was a curious impression of deep menace which each of the travelers felt at the same moment.

"Perhaps," Abna ventured, "it was just an illusion—a trick of the light."

"It wasn't!" Viona protested heatedly. "I tell you—"

"No, it was not an illusion," came Vashon's deep voice, and he sounded strangely resigned. "This is a misfit planet, my friends, mysteriously cursed by not conforming to natural law. It is a world that doesn't evolve naturally from birth to death, and enjoy the happiness or sorrow that lies in that path. Instead, it is out of step with the universe. It leaps ahead into time at unexpected moments, thereby suddenly accumulating many years of age and ruin—and killing tens of thousands of people, because old age and death catch up on them during the transition. Such a leap did happen a little while ago. At any moment another leap might come—and it would involve you, too. You would die, because you would abruptly leap ahead beyond the span of your life."

"You were here when this last leap occurred?" the Amazon asked presently.

"I was."

"Yet you did not die? Or evolve?"

"I am the ruler," came the tired response. "Because of that I must be—and am—preserved. Sazner here, with his scientific skill, is always able to forecast when a leap will come. He then hurries me and certain other important dignitaries to his laboratory, where we are isolated until the leap has come and gone. The forces he controls prevent the time-leap affecting us. He himself travels into space to investigate."

The Amazon's violet eyes turned to the scarlet-colored adviser.

"I am surprised, Sazner, that a being of your scientific skill—who can evidently make time stand still for your king and his contemporaries—cannot overcome the main fault in the planet itself. Surely it is only a question of cosmic mathematics."

"There are far more factors involved than that," was Sazner's acid response. "And in any event I do not propose to discuss the problem with outer-space visitors. We have our problems, as you have yours. Shall we let it stay that way?"

The Amazon glanced at Abna and for an instant she seemed on the verge of a hot retort. Then she checked herself.

"How long," the ruler asked, glancing at Sazner, "do you think it will be before another leap takes place? I would not like our friends to be involved in anything that might cause them harm."

"According to my calculations, Excellency, there will be no more trouble for some time to come."

"Good!" There was relief in the ruler's bass voice. "In that case, my friends, you must attend a celebration banquet when we can discuss our differing forms of life and pursuits. I will see to it that a suite is placed at your disposal, and we will dine at nightfall. Does that meet with your approval?"

"Decidedly, Excellency," Abna smiled.

The ruler turned aside and crossed to a bell-push. It was only a matter of moments before a pale blue being came in and waited respectfully. He absorbed the weird sounds that came from his ruler, then the door was held wide and, Abna in the lead, the travelers passed out into the huge main hall and eventually found themselves in a resplendent suite of rooms where not one bit of furniture was the slightest use to them. But at least they were to themselves, and that was something.

CHAPTER THREE
ATTEMPTED MURDER

"There is one definite thing I do know," Viona said, as she tidied herself up as best she could, "and that is that I don't like our red friend—Sazner. His very voice hurts."

"And Vashon is completely under his influence," Abna mused. "Or do I imagine it?"

"Not for a moment," the Amazon told him, pacing slowly up and down and musing. "We've dropped smack in the middle of an interesting scientific problem, Abna, and we're up against minds—or at least one mind in particular—of tremendous scientific skill. Meaning Sazner, of course. He's up to something: I'm sure of it, and the thing he resents most is our arrival."

"Anyway, I'm glad I've proved I didn't imagine that leap-frog stunt," Viona exclaimed. "And incidentally, what do you suppose causes it? How can a world suddenly jump in time? It's contrary to all natural scientific law."

"Of course it is," the Amazon confirmed. "But Vashon seems to think it's a freak of Nature. It isn't—and never could be. A thing like that could only happen by applied celestial mechanics, and the one person—far as we know so far—who could do that is Sazner. Yes, indeed, we face an interesting little problem."

There were no further moves until the blazing sun was dipping behind the strange buildings; then an escort of four arrived and stood in drooped but quivering respect in the wide doorway. One of them appeared to speak.

"His Excellency presents his greetings and trusts that you will now join him in an official banquet. Kindly come with us."

The four obeyed without comment, eventually finding themselves in an enormous dining hall down the center of which was a table of usual height, the curly-type chairs being placed all around it. Some of the guests had already assembled, but the head of the table, where Vashon would presumably sit, was empty at the moment.

"What happens if their food is poisonous to us?" the Amazon asked, as Abna walked beside her. "If we refuse to eat it will be an insult."

"We'll have to explain our refusal, that's all," Abna shrugged. "We're certainly not going to poison ourselves to please Vashon or anybody else. For myself, I'll be intrigued to see how these beings eat at all, with no recognizable mouths or faces. And as for these chairs, we'll have to perch against them as best we can."

This they did, trying to appear as dignified as possible under the awkward conditions—then at length

Vashon appeared, accompanied as usual by the scarlet scientist at his right side.

There was merely a formal exchange of greetings and then the servants brought forth the food. Apparently Vashon had worked out everything in advance because the solid food was placed before the travelers—and extremely palatable it looked—and a different type of food was assigned to the tulip people. This seemed to be some kind of mess, which looked like paste.

"As near as possible, from a reading of your minds, I have endeavored to provide sustenance suitable to you," Vashon explained. "It is synthetically created since, of course, we have no animals on this world which could be slain to provide meat. I trust you will bear with me in the difficulty."

"We are honored," the Amazon murmured, and though she had the feeling she was perhaps taking her life in her hands she began her meal. To her surprise it was quite delicious.

"Might I ask," Sazner questioned, when the meal was under way, "how long you intend to remain with us?"

"We have no plans in that direction," Abna replied. "Naturally we don't wish to trespass upon your hospitality, but on the other hand, we would like the fullest exchange of information. This time-leaping planet fascinates us quite a deal."

"After we have dined you must see our major laboratory," Vashon suggested. "I myself am not particularly well versed in science, but I am sure Sazner will have no objection to showing you some of our marvels."

Sazner's featureless face turned slightly to the ruler. "As you wish, Excellency. If you think it desirable."

There was an awkward silence, which Vashon himself broke.

"That is my request, Sazner, and you will kindly comply."

The chief scientist said no more, but there was yet again that hint of enmity in the air. Not that the four Crusaders paid much attention to it: they were much more interested in discovering how these queer beings nourished themselves. It appeared that the method was to convey the paste food to an orifice near the top of the stalk-like body, which orifice operated in exactly the same way as a normal human mouth. At first sight it was astonishing, then like everything else, familiarity began to breed contempt and it was no longer intriguing.

"We would be willing to try to help you overcome your problem if you wish it," Abna said, and at the ruler seemed to hesitate. It was while he did so that Sazner cut in.

"Everything that can be done to overcome this fault is being done. I am the leading scientist and I have the problem under careful observation. Each time my calculations show that a time-leap is due, I travel into space to watch the effect and make the necessary calculations from it. Also during this time, as you are aware, His Excellency and certain of these other dignitaries are saved from disaster by residing in my laboratory."

"Since there is still a population of sorts, thin though it seems to be," the Amazon continued, "I assume that these time-leaps do not involve everybody?"

"That depends on the extent of the leap," Sazner answered. "As a rule a jump of fifty years is the common thing, therefore the people who survive are those who were young people at the moment of the leap. When the leap is over they are fifty years further along their lives—and so is everything else. So far there has not been a case of a jump covering thousands of years, otherwise the entire race would automatically vanish, except for those protected in the laboratory."

"I am still sure," Abna said deliberately, "that it is only a problem in mathematics which can be solved, thereby giving back this planet its rightful heritage."

"I am well able to take care of the situation," Sazner commented acidly.

In perhaps another half-hour the banquet was over. Outside, the night was intense even though the city itself was brightly illuminated. The meal ended, Vashon arose from his curled support, and every member present rose also.

"I have a number of matters to attend to," he said, "so I will hand you over now to Sazner. I am sure he will show you the laboratories, and answer any questions you may care to ask."

"Certainly, Excellency," came Sazner's cold assent, and with that he turned and led the way to the door with the travelers coming up behind him.

Once within the main laboratory, situated somewhere deep underneath the official building, the four had to admit that it was remarkably well supplied with instruments and machines. Some of them made sense, but a great number did not—nor did Sazner seem particularly inclined to explain anything as he led the way down the main gangways, glancing occasionally at the tulip people who were tending the humming machines.

"I assume this is also the source of the city's power?" the Amazon asked presently.

"Certainly. This is the heart of the city where light and power are generated. The basis of our power is atomic energy."

This was not unexpected, but it made Abna suddenly pause.

"Atomic power? Everything here is generated from that source?"

"It is," agreed the cold voice.

"Then we have to take certain precautions," Abna said. "Our constitution is such that we dare not expose it to radioactivity without disastrous consequences. True, we have the mastery of mind over matter in certain cases, but that involves such a tremendous mental effort it is not worth it if normal precautions can be taken. Before we go farther, Sazner, we need insulated suits."

"I see." Apparently this was causing the scientist some surprise. "We ourselves are not in the least affected by atomic radiation, so the possibility of your being so never occurred to me.... I suppose there must be many things which are fatal to you but not to us."

"Certain forms of radiation, heat, cold, gases," the Amazon said. "Many of them are lethal to our constitution. For instance, I imagine from your constitution that chlorine gas would not affect you unduly, though it might be uncomfortable."

"No more than an unpleasant odor," Sazner replied.

"But to us—death," the Amazon shrugged. "Such is the difference in our constitutions."

Sazner appeared to reflect further; then he came to a decision.

"To prepare insulated suits for you at a moment's notice is impossible, so it would be as well to postpone this laboratory tour until later, when I've made the necessary arrangements.... It would be much safer for you to leave. This place is full of radioactivity."

On the face of it, it seemed the most sensible thing to do, so within ten minutes the quartet found themselves back again in their suite—and to their surprise, makeshift beds of huge piled cushions had been provided, the nearest approach the tulip people could provide to a normal bed.

"How did things look to you with Sazner?" Abna asked, as the four of them sprawled amongst the cushions and relaxed.

"To my mind," the Amazon responded thoughtfully, "he seemed extremely glad of the opportunity for an excuse to be rid of us. If he repeats the offer to see the laboratories, and provides us with insulated suits, nobody will be more surprised than I."

"They're strange beings whichever way you look at them," Mexone commented. "Vegetable basis and unaffected by radioactivity and the things that hurt us most An almost impossible race to understand."

"For the moment," Abna told him, "there is little we can do without precipitating open hostility. Sazner is dead against any interference on our part—so we'll have to watch for our opportunity. The longer we're here, the more we learn, and the moment we get the chance, we'll act."

The effects of the meal, and the quality of the atmosphere combined quickly to plunge the quartet into deep sleep almost before they realized it. Even the fact that the lights were on did not bother them—and as they slept, things began to happen.

It appeared first as a wispy vapor floating through the ventilator grille set midway up the main wall. After a moment it increased in density, until it was commencing to fill the room with fine mist. Nor could it escape. The windows were tightly shut and the base of the door had a trap upon it, which brought it flush with the floor. So, gradually, the fog deepened, until at length the quartet began to move uneasily in their slumber.

It was the Amazon who awakened first, when the vapors had deepened so much as to nearly obscure the lighting. The instant her eyes opened, they smarted abominably and she dragged frantically at breath that seemed to scorch her lungs. It only took her a few seconds to determine what had happened—that lethal gas was being pumped into the room. Probably—in fact certainly—all four of them would by this time have died in their sleep but for their tremendous physical strength.

As it was, the Amazon struggled up with enormous effort from the cushions. She shook Abna, Viona, and Mexone each in turn, and then essayed another effort that got her to her feet. Swaying dizzily, she stared around her in the fog, then stumbled to where she believed she had seen the window.

Her guess was right. She slammed her elbow against the glass, but to her horror the glass did not break. It was composed of some kind of transparent material as hard as steel.

"Smash it!" Viona choked, struggling forward. "Smash—the window...." She reeled helplessly, clutching at her throat. "This—this stuff's...chlorine gas!"

Frantically the Amazon tried again, this time with her flame gun—but even this deadly weapon had no impression.

"The door!" came Abna's strangled voice. "Only way...."

There was a dim vision of his huge form moving blurrily, then Viona collapsed completely. The Amazon made a desperate struggle to keep her senses, but even she failed and tumbled helplessly across her daughter. Only Abna and Mexone remained standing, holding their breath against the gas, and fighting inch by inch to gain the door.

Abna got to it first and with his remaining strength pulled savagely on the handle. When the door refused to budge he yanked out his protonic gun and shattered the lock. Only then did the portal swing outwards.

Only just in possession of their senses, both men reeled out into the deserted, well-lighted corridor beyond, and there they remained for a moment while they drew clear air into their lungs. Steadied somewhat, they turned about and plunged back into the room, searching through the fog until they came to the fallen Amazon and Viona.

The rest was simple. Abna whipped up the Amazon, and Mexone lifted Viona into his arms. Once in the clear air of the corridor both women quickly began to revive—and the annoyance that came to the Amazon's face when she realized what had happened was obvious.

"No need to reproach yourself," Abna told her, as she gained her feet and stood breathing hard. "Superhuman or otherwise, the female is always more susceptible to poisoning than the male. It isn't that that matters; it's the one who's done his best to try to finish us."

"Sazner, naturally!" the Amazon snapped, whipping her proton gun out of her belt. "That gas was chlorine vapor, forced through the ventilator shaft—and nobody but Sazner knows that chlorine gas is fatal to us. I'm not waiting for opportunities any more, Abna. I'm tackling Sazner right now!"

"I suggest, m'dear, that we view the thing logically," said Abna. "We have weapons between us, such as they are, but Sazner has a whole laboratory at his disposal, together with scientific skill. If we precipitate an open conflict with him we'll get the worst of it! Subtlety is our greatest weapon, and we've got to use it. Now we know from this attack that we're not exactly welcome on this planet—at least as far as Sazner is concerned. We're going back in our room the moment the air has cleared, and for the rest of the night one of us will remain on guard. Tomorrow we say absolutely nothing about it."

The Amazon's yellow fingers twitched on the butt of her flame gun. She surveyed the deserted expanse.

"May be your idea of things, Abna, but it isn't mine. Since Sazner has failed in one direction, he'll try in another, so we ought to pull his cork before he gets the chance."

But Abna was adamant, so finally for the sake of peace the Amazon fell in with his suggestion. When at length the gas had ceased pouring into the suite and the air was clear of it, they returned to the room, patched up the broken lock, and all but the Amazon herself resumed their positions on the cushions.

"I'll stay on guard," she volunteered. "I'm hoping that maybe Sazner will come along and see what's happened. If he does, he'll get something to remember me by."

But evidently Sazner was not so precipitate as that, for there was no sign of him during the rest of the night. A disgruntled Amazon was still beside the door as daylight returned and she gave Abna a grim look as he awakened from sleep.

"Still determined not to mention the attack?" she asked bitterly.

"Still determined," Abna confirmed, rising.

"For myself," the Amazon said, coming forward, "I think this cat-and-mouse business we're playing is too confining. To say nothing of dangerous. We'd do better if we—"

She broke off as the broken door suddenly opened and none other than Vashon, the ruler, entered. He was alone. His odd tulip head glanced around, and presumably whatever organs he used for sight picked up the scene immediately.

"I am much relieved to find that all is well with you," he said, obvious concern in his voice.

"May I ask what else you expected?" Abna asked dryly.

"I expected, my friend, that perhaps Sazner might have made some attempt to be rid of you. I was not able to speak to you on the matter yesterday because he was constantly beside me, but I was determined I would rise at an early time this morning and contact you." Vashon moved farther into the room and dropped his voice. "For the sake of your own safety I would advise you to leave this planet, though I personally could wish nothing better than that you would stay."

"For your information," the Amazon said, "Sazner made an effort to kill us in the night by chlorine gas, and but for our strong physiques we would have become extinguished in our sleep. Notice the door? We had to smash our way out."

Vashon's flower-like head turned in that direction, then back to the group.

"You would save a great deal of trouble if you would depart, my friends, apparently of your own volition. It does not pay me to quarrel with Sazner because he is far too clever a scientist—"

"Ruining your planet for reasons unknown," Viona put in, her face grim.

"No, child. He is doing his utmost to save things—of that I am sure. But he resents intruders and you would be safer away. I beg of you to leave."

The Amazon came forward. "Look, Excellency, you do not think for one moment that Sazner is trying to help you, do you?"

"But of course he is! He works constantly on the problem of the time-leaps, and does he not protect me and the dignitaries whenever a time-leap is due?"

"Did it ever occur to you," Abna asked, "that the time-leaps might be the work of Sazner himself?"

The ruler was silent for a moment or two, his slight movements betraying his hesitation. Finally he asked a question. It was a plaintive one, typical of a man surrounded by forces he is incapable of controlling.

"I am not a scientist, my friends, and never have been. We of this world are not particularly advanced in that direction. We rely on Sazner and his army of helpers for all the scientific progress we make—such as radio, space travel, and so forth. Now you suggest Sazner may be working to annihilate us. How do I make sure of that fact? More important still, what do I do about it?"

"To preserve yourself for the time being there is nothing you can do," the Amazon responded. "But we can. We have the measure of Sazner very nicely, and if we can possibly free you from his influence we shall do so. As for the scientific side, we know quite as many tricks as Sazner himself—probably more—and when you are freed from his influence, we'll hand them over to you.... But we must work carefully, and do not question for a moment whatever decisions we make."

"Very well...." Bewilderment was there now. "But—but who are you, my friends? You are different from any beings I have ever seen before."

"We call ourselves the Cosmic Crusaders," Abna said quietly. "All of us are scientists, from far distant worlds, joined together in the common bond of scientific unity, and determined to help the races of those worlds who need us.... Tell me, Excellency, is Sazner a member of your own race?"

"As far as I know, he is. But not of this particular country. There are many countries on this planet, and from his coloration I think he belongs to the Exodian race to the north of the planet. They have that same distinctive scarlet hue. He brought his scientific skill to my notice some years ago when the first time-leaps began to happen, so I accepted his offer of becoming our master-scientist. Not just for my particular race but the whole planet."

There was a brief silence; then Vashon 'spoke' again.

"I must not delay here any longer, my friends. I trust

you will honor me with your presence at the first meal of the day. I will send a guard to escort you."

With that he departed. The four looked at each other, but did not exchange any comments: they had too much to think about for that. They freshened themselves up as best they could with the limited amenities around them and then walked with the escort to the dining hall. This time there was no suggestion of the previous night's opulent banquet—just the ruler himself at the long table, several others who perhaps were his family, and inevitably the scarlet-hued body of Sazner himself.

What exactly Sazner's emotions were on beholding the four alive and well it was impossible to tell.

Vashon made a statement.

"I have disturbing news for you, my friends. Sazner has just informed me that another time-leap—unexpectedly soon after the other one—is due almost any time. Immediately after we have finished this meal, I am going with my family and contemporaries to have the usual protection of the laboratory—but that facility does not extend to any of you. Your physique is so different from ours it would be impossible to work out the necessary details in time."

"Well, then, what happens?" the Amazon demanded. "Are we to assume that we'll be involved in this time-leap when it comes?"

"Certainly you will be," Sazner responded. "It will age all of you by many years—perhaps even kill you altogether. Your only alternative is to leave the planet."

"Time we went, Vi," Abna snapped, with a glance at

the Amazon. "Nothing of useful purpose can be served by staying on this planet. Our regrets, Excellency, on this abrupt departure, but we did warn you not to question whatever decisions we might make."

"Yes," Vashon admitted, in regret. "You did."

Abna jerked his head in command and the Amazon rose and crossed to his side. Viona and Mexone automatically did the same thing and in silence they left the great room.

CHAPTER FOUR
PLANET OF MONSTERS

"Just what are we going to do?" Viona asked, bewildered. "We can't keep tabs on anything if we leave the planet."

"On the contrary, Viona, I think we can," Abna said. "I just remembered something. It may be wrong; it may be right, but we did see a spaceship descending a little while after the last time-leap, and we also know that Sazner presumably leaps into space to 'study' the problem whenever there's a time-leap due. He leaves Vashon and his contemporaries safe and then absents himself. I'll take a guess and say that he goes somewhere to cause the time-leaps to happen, returning afterwards when all is safe. In that way he avoids being involved in the leap itself."

"Yes, sounds possible," the Amazon admitted. "Meaning, I suppose, that the spaceship we saw arriving was Sazner coming home?"

"Exactly. He'd never keep scientific machinery of such importance and secrecy on this planet: it must be elsewhere, and the sooner we discover where, the better. I'll go one step further and say that he doesn't belong to this planet at all, in spite of Vashon's statements."

None of them spoke again until the *Ultra* was reached, and rather to their surprise they found that nothing had been interfered with. Somehow they had had the uneasy conviction that Sazner would have attempted some kind of sabotage—but if indeed he had tried anything of this nature, the negative energy flowing from the vessel, making it impenetrable except by those who understood it, had beaten him.

This time it was Abna who moved to the main control board, and as she depressed the switch that closed the airlock, the Amazon gave him a questioning glance.

"Well, what do we do? The *Ultra* isn't an easy vessel to conceal. Sazner is bound to see us when we go into space and he does the same thing."

"Not at a million miles he won't, and our radar-x instruments are easily sensitive at that range. We'll hop out of sight and then train the radar on him and watch what he does."

"Check," the Amazon agreed, and with that Abna switched on the mighty power plant.

In a matter of moments the huge vessel was sweeping upwards into the morning sunlight. In less than a minute from departure the atmospheric belt had been traversed and the black of space yawned ahead. Abna stepped up the power gradually until the *Ultra* was flashing at incredible speed through the void, leaving the leap-frog world far behind: then at a million miles distance he slowed down, and gradually came to a virtual stop, except for the gentle pulls of the other planets in the system.

"Radar's okay," Mexone said, turning from where he and Viona had been busy adjusting it. "The moment Sazner pokes his nose into space we'll pick it up."

Abna nodded in satisfaction and then thoughtfully contemplated the other five worlds of this particular system.

"One of those is probably the answer," he said finally. "One of them must carry the scientific machinery which Sazner uses. Once we know the answer to that, there's much we can do."

"Such as?" the Amazon questioned.

"Well, we could blow his machinery, and the planet itself, to smithereens, if we chose."

"We could do something simpler and more effective than that," the Amazon declared. "Why, when we know he's in space, don't we attack him with everything we've got and blow him right out of the system? Finish him for good?"

"Because, my dear impetuous Vi, he may not be alone in this scheme, and if others carried on where he'd been compelled to leave off, where would we be? No. Smash him and his machinery—and anybody else connected with it before we—"

"He's starting off now!" Viona cut in eagerly. "Look at the screen!"

Abna turned. There, plain enough and looking very much like a movie in negative, was a view of the right-hand limb of the leap-frog world, and just beyond it a slowly moving dot. This was radar of the most advanced design, almost telescopic in its qualities and contrived so that space appeared white and anything against it black. By such a means tracking was simplified.

"We don't need to watch any longer," Abna said surveying space from the window. "From the direction he's taking, that nearest planet is obviously his destination. There's nowhere else he can be going. Time to get on the move, approach that planet from the rear, and then open up on him with everything we've got."

On the face of it, the plan seemed simple and perfect, but all four glanced at each other when, about an hour later, Abna brought the *Ultra* into the final run which would normally have carried the vessel straight to its destination. It had become suddenly obvious that something was wrong, for instead of sweeping irresistibly forward, the *Ultra* was jolting and jumping violently as though being hit by pockets of air. Such a possibility in outer space was immediately written off, but there had to be some kind of explanation

"Maybe Sazner's cleverer than we thought," Abna muttered. "If he's seen us and has machinery powerful enough, he can perhaps cause us plenty of trouble—"

"What's happening?" Viona demanded, turning a startled face from the secondary window.

"No idea," the Amazon snapped, frowning anxiously. "I would have said that the *Ultra* was capable of smashing through any known barrier, but this is something different. We're being manipulated by radio control, or something."

"This is no radio control," Abna told her. "It's something far more overwhelming. Offhand I'd say gravitational stresses or something—the force of a whole planet—is being turned against us. We just haven't enough power in the ship to cope with it."

"Obviously, it's Sazner at work," the Amazon said. "He must have seen us coming and set to work to drive us away—and very effectively he's doing it." There was a trace of admiration in her voice. "Here's a scientist well worthy of our attention, Abna. He can control the very elemental forces of the universe itself."

"I doubt if he has such resources on his own ship," Abna said, thinking. "Having spotted us, he's probably contacted scientists on his own planet by radio, and they are doing it by projecting a—" he broke off suddenly and pointed.

"Unless we think of something quickly, we'll not get much chance to fight him," Abna added. "Take a look where we're going! We're being diverted to that planet ahead, the outermost one in this system."

"Abna, we've got to do something," the Amazon said abruptly, studying the instruments. "Far from decreasing speed, we're gaining velocity with every second, and now it is being augmented by the gravitational pull of that planet we're headed for."

Abna crossed to her side and Viona and Mexone carne up behind him. The vast urgency of the situation had by now been completely forced upon them.

"We're already beyond safety limit," the Amazon said, with a quick glance. "Even to start slowing down will hardly be enough. Just what sort of power can Sazner be using?"

"I've been thinking about that," Abna responded, completely calm. "I don't believe it's a thrust at all, otherwise its influence wouldn't extend so far. What he—or more likely scientists on his home world—has probably done is create a warp in space along the track the *Ultra* is following. Since one can only fly through space in a straight line, it wouldn't be difficult for him. That warp, in trying to snap back into place, like a piece of elastic pulled to the maximum, carries everything else along with it with irresistible power, including us. Our solution is not to try to overcome the trouble by stopping ourselves—which we'd never be able to do—but by rotating ourselves right out of the warp into normal space. Rather like catapulting ourselves out of a stupendously fast river to the normal bank at the side of it. We're in the midst of a kind of invisible spatial sluice."

"All very interesting," the Amazon said anxiously, "but how do we get out? I thought I knew every trick with this vessel of mine—but rotating into a new space is a new one. I just haven't the time to work it out."

"I've already done it," Abna said, unshaken. "All our power has to be concentrated to one side, not at the front or rear. We have emergency side rockets, and that's where we want the power. Either side will do. Take the right, to begin with."

Mystified, even slightly annoyed that her own scientific skill was not the equal of Abna's, the Amazon stood to one side and gave him full command of the switch panel.

The result was astonishing. The *Ultra* jolted, lunged, and then actually rolled over and over. All four were thrown from their feet and hit the walls. Fortunately, the heavy padding saved them from injury, but by the time the great vessel had ceased its wild gyrations none of them knew which was up or down. They struggled to their feet, looked around them, and found that at least the ceiling was up and the floor down.

"Apparently you did it," the Amazon confessed grudgingly.

Abna dived for the control panel and snapped the switches back into the normal positions; then he began to start up the power plant once more, this time feeding the front jets. The effect this time was immediate. The vessel was under full control.

"You still can't turn aside?" The Amazon turned quickly from the big window, where she had been gazing out with Viona and Mexone.

"Not yet. I'm doing everything I dare risk." Abna made a further study of the instruments and his face became serious. "I don't think we can turn aside in time. All I can do on the last drop is give the forward jets everything they've got and we'll have to risk a crash landing. Better prepare for it."

A sense of devastating headlong falling was upon each of them, and it ended in a sudden smashing jolt, which sent them reeling backwards to the padded floor. The *Ultra* had stopped moving, but had driven itself deep into something yielding, and thereby saved itself from a savage battering. For several moments it hung with tail upraised, then settled down dizzily. From outside there came a dull sucking squelch.

Abna was the first on his feet. He hurried over to the window and then stood gazing in amazement. He had no need of comment. The others, as they joined him, could see for themselves exactly what kind of a world they had landed in. Immediately ahead of them was forest, but of such staggering proportions it was almost unbelievable. Tree trunks at least 200 feet wide at the base speared themselves upwards until they were lost in the swirling clouds. Laced between the trees, in fantastic designs, were all manner of vines, lichens, and even what appeared to be monstrous cobweb fili-grees, though what kind of a spider it could have been that had weaved such designs defied imagination.

"Only one solution," Abna said at length. "Have to pump the bog dry, clean out the jets, and then take off. Going to take some time, so the sooner we start the better. What sort of conditions have we got outside?"

He looked at the instruments. The readings showed that the atmosphere was breathable but extremely damp. Temperatures ranged around the eighty degree F. mark. Gravitation was similar to that of Earth.

"All right," Abna said, turning. "Let's get busy."

He fitted the pumping apparatus with a long length of hose, then opened the airlock. For a moment he sniffed the heavy, warm air, then clambered outside, the hose around his broad shoulders. Carefully he tested his weight on the oozing bog, shook his head, and withdrew his foot.

"Can't stand on that," he pronounced, glancing back at the Amazon, Viona, and Mexone as they watched him. "Have to work from the top of the *Ultra*, that's all."

Viona pressed the switch that ejected an emergency ladder from the vessel's side, and Abna climbed it swiftly. After a moment the Amazon and Mexone followed him, Viona staying behind to control the pumping apparatus, which was connected to the power plant. Then, carefully, Abna lowered the hose and ejector head into the swamp and adjusted the wide funnel up which the swamp mud and water would come.

"That should do it," he said finally. "It'll hurl the mud and water 100 feet away, where it should go down that slope away from us. Just as long as we can get enough water out to get down to the jets— Right, Viona!" he shouted, and inside the control room she switched on the power.

At the same moment as the plant started up with its dull hum of energy there was also another sound, audible even above the hissing splosh of water and mud now sailing away into distance out of the swamp. This new sound made Abna, the Amazon, and Mexone all glance up sharply and look around them. It was a thin, high, buzzing note, very like a rapid buzz-saw, and with the seconds it became louder.

"That the pump mechanism, or—" The Amazon

stopped dead, staring into the forest; then she clutched Abna's arm and pointed. He and Mexone both saw it at the same moment. It had no particular classification since it was shaped like a shuttle and sprouted tiny wings. These wings were a mere haze, and it was their terrific vibration that caused the buzz-saw note.

"It's a beetle, or a wasp, or something!" Abna gasped. "And eight feet long at least—"

"Got a beak like a swordfish," Mexone gasped out, tugging his gun free and leveling it. "One jab from that could cut us in two— *Look out!*"

With a screaming whine the flying atrocity dived again, much lower this time. Abna had no time to dodge since he was in the midst of shifting the pump hosing. The Amazon glanced at him from where she had thrown herself flat and tried to pull her gun. This much she managed, but had no chance to sight it. Then Mexone fired his own weapon, crouched as he was on one knee immediately to one side of Abna. The sizzling needle-thin flame ripped with livid fire straight down the underneath of the horror's body. It emitted a scream that nearly burst the eardrums and then split in two halves, which sailed either side of Abna and then dropped in the swamp.

"That," Mexone whispered, sweat streaming down his face; "was close! Too close."

"Good work," Abna said, clapping his shoulder. "I just had no time to pull myself out of that one. The—"

He paused, staring at the hose. After a moment he pulled up a ragged end. It had only just dawned on him that the mud and water was no longer being pumped away. All that was happening was a tremendous boiling below surface.

"Cut the power!" he yelled to Viona, and she obeyed. Then her somewhat frightened face presently appeared as she half climbed the ladder.

"What in heaven's name was that thing?" she demanded. "I just couldn't do anything. It scared the life out of me."

"Flying buzz-saw or something," Abna told her briefly. "And even though it didn't kill us, it's done other damage. Look at this hose! Cut clean in two!"

Incredulously the others stared at the dangling end in Abna's hand. In dropping, evidently, the horror's saw-snout had cleaved through the hose.

There was silence for a moment as once again this small problem took on the proportions of a large one. The only possible apparatus for draining the swamp was irretrievably lost, and unless the jets were cleared, the vessel could not possibly get on the move.

"We've got diving kit," the Amazon said at length. "Suppose we went down into the swamp and.... No, wouldn't do," she admitted, as Abna gave her a dubious glance.

"Perhaps—" Viona began to suggest, and then she broke off at a distant crashing reverberation. Expectantly—their guns drawn and ready this time— the four looked about them, and as the noise continued, it was not long before the source of it became apparent.

Approaching through the forest, smashing tree

branches as it advanced, was quite the most stupendous creature the four had ever seen. It was right beyond the usual class of dinosauria and gargantua: it was huge in every sense of the word, towering up to nearly 200 feet at the top of its horn-ridged back.

"What is it?" Mexone asked faintly.

"Dunno," Abna muttered, staring at it. "We certainly can't fight it with these flame guns. Quick, back into the ship. We can perhaps train a cannon on it."

One by one the four tumbled into the control room and then shut the airlock. The Amazon raced for the armament and the others dived for the window. All they could see now were two colossal gray-skinned legs, quite four feet across, and at the top of them somewhere was the monster's body.

CHAPTER FIVE
DUEL WITH COLOSSUS

"Let him have it, Vi," Abna said briefly. "If he makes up his mind to tramp forward he'll crush the *Ultra*'s armor plate like an eggshell."

The Amazon did not answer. She was frantically trying to maneuver the big proton gun into position—the biggest weapon in the *Ultra*'s armory, but the angle was so difficult she finally had to give up.

"Can't be done," she said finally, glancing. "Have to try something else."

"For instance?" Viona asked.

There was a second or two while they all endeavored to think of a way around the difficulty, and in those seconds the monster acted for itself.

Presumably it had seized hold of one of the exterior projections with its mouth, for the *Ultra* suddenly began to rock and sway violently. Abna was about to speak when a violent lurch sent him reeling backwards. He hit the wall and slid to the floor, the others beside him. Viona, the first up and nearest the window, flung herself towards it.

"We're moving!" she gasped, her startled face

pressed again the glass. "He's carrying the whole ship in his mouth!"

"Suppose," the Amazon said, thinking, "we detached the proton gun from its mountings and carried it outside? On to the deck? We couldn't miss that way."

It was a daring proposition, yet probably the only one in this desperate extremity. Abna pondered it for only a moment and then he nodded.

"Right! We'll risk it."

There was no further delay. In a matter of moments the heavy gun was released from its mountings and Abna fastened it over his massive shoulders. The separate control panel was also detached, leaving a long extension power cable.

The Amazon opened the airlock, shouldered the heavy panel, and then gave Abna the nod. He turned to Viona and Mexone.

"You two stay and control the power," he said. "We'll do the rest." With that he stepped through the airlock and swung around to mount the ladder to the deck.

Within a moment or two Abna had reached the swaying, flat top of the vessel and tugged the heavy gun from his shoulder. By the time he got it fixed on its emergency tripod, the Amazon had also climbed up. She laid the panel down flat and then squatted for action, meanwhile staring at the great wall of wrinkled gray skin which formed the brute's inconceivably big upper jaw.... The eyes were just visible now, too—as big as dinner plates and protected by horny rims.

"Certainly he's an outsize," Abna muttered, also

surveying as he angled the gun. "You okay with the switch panel, Vi?"

"Uh-huh. Any moment you say."

Abna put his hand on the starting switch and then thought for a moment.

"Be prepared for a heavy jolt," he warned. "This creature will drop the ship like as not when he gets the gunfire.... Full power down there!" he yelled, and at the sound of his voice the monster seemed to hesitate for a moment and then went crashing onwards again through the forest.

"Power full." the Amazon announced, watching the panel.

Abna pressed the button, directing the savage, destructive energy straight at the great wall of neck in front of him. Yet here was the strange thing. This protonic energy, which on more than one occasion had blown armor-plated spaceships into dust, made not the least impression on this giant of a satanic world. There was no smoke, no lunge of pain from the creature, just nothing at all.

"I wonder...," Abna breathed, and looked at Amazon with a gleam in his eves.

"Wonder what?" She sounded irritated.

"It's the only way," Abna decided. "Mental compulsion. I'll see if I can't force the brute to drop us. I'll have to climb on to his snout so I can see his eyes. The eyes are the direct communication to the brain."

The Amazon did not say anything because she was too astonished. Then Abna added: "Get Viona and

Mexone below. If I succeed in this, you'll all have to get to work cleaning the jets while I keep the brute at bay. Hurry it up."

The Amazon wasted no more time. Neither did Abna. He walked to the point where the huge upper jaw was clamped around the spaceship, and then began to muscle himself up on to the rubbery snout. Before long he was directly facing those enormous pools of eyes. It was impossible to read anything in them but brute ferocity and, perhaps, a certain deep-down fear.

It seemed an intolerable time before anything happened, but at last the brute began to slow down, and at length came to a complete standstill. The only sounds were those of the rustling leaves of the forest and the snorting breath of the giant. Abna still did not move. He typified, in those moments, the complete control of man over beast—and, very gradually, the stupendous head at last began to lower.

"He's doing it," the Amazon whispered. "Stand by."

She was right. The monster was by this time completely under Abna's mental subjugation. The *Ultra* was lowered to the ground and the vast jaws unclamped from around it. Abna, still perched on the great snout, remained where he was, swinging upwards dizzily as the beast raised its head up again. From a great distance the voice of the Amazon came floating.

"We'll clear the jets and then raise the *Ultra* to pick you off. Hang on as long as you can."

Abna clung on desperately to the broad snout, his hands clutching into the folds of iron-gray skin. Twice he was nearly thrown off, but held on by the sheer strength of his muscles. To the rear, as the brute blundered on, smashing down trees and branches with juggernaut impact, came the low-flying *Ultra*. The Amazon herself was controlling it, and it demanded every dodge and trick she knew to steer at such a low level amid close-neighbored trees and at hardly a trickle of power.

So the maneuvering and dodging continued until a clearing began to appear in the distance. Immediately the Amazon shot the *Ultra* towards it.

"Drop the grapples," she ordered, glancing at Viona. "See that they close around your father the moment we pass over him."

"Right!" Viona answered promptly, and made the necessary preparations while the Amazon swung the vessel right and left at a height perhaps fifty feet above that of the monster.

The timing was exactly right. Just as the brute came into the clearing the *Ultra* swept diagonally across it, the grapples swinging through the air. They locked around Abna's arms and legs and lifted him free. Instantly the Amazon changed the *Ultra*'s course to the vertical and Abna found himself swinging in mid-air high above the forest. After which the thing was simple. The grapples were withdrawn on the electric winch and Abna finally tumbled into the control room.

"Never a dull moment," he commented, standing up and shaking the grapples free. "Thanks. That was a nice piece of work. Riding that hobby-horse once I'd lost control wasn't my idea of fun at all."

The Amazon depressed the airlock button and then put on the power. With ever-increasing speed the *Ultra* began to move away from the crazy outermost world until at last it was in the yawning emptiness of outer space. Only then did the Amazon switch in the automatic control. This done, she moved to where Abna was seated with Viona and Mexone by the window.

"What I don't understand," the Amazon said, thinking, "is why Sazner forces the planet ahead in jumps, and then stops for a time. Why do that? Since he obviously must have an ultimate object, it surely would be more sensible to make one big leap and finish the job? Why does he protract the issue?"

Abna shrugged. "That's an unanswered question. May be quite a few reasons for it."

"The only ones who are not gaining anything out of this lot are ourselves," Mexone put in. "What have we had so far? Near-suffocation by chlorine gas, and an attempt to murder us on the world we've just left. For Crusaders, we're not doing wonderfully well."

"There'll be action aplenty once we know what we're really fighting," Viona said promptly. "And come to think of it, we may have gained something by being flung to the outermost world. I think it can be considered a possibility that Sazner probably thinks we're all dead by now—and that belief gives us freedom of action without any attempts to destroy us."

"Yes, you're right enough there," the Amazon agreed: then she looked at Abna. "I think we ought to take advantage of our so-called deaths and fly back as quickly as possible to have a word with Vashon alone. So far he's never had a chance to speak to us without Sazner being nearby, which must have cramped his style. Sazner may not be returning to the leap-frog world just yet a while. We can do a lot of good if we get ahead of him."

Her mind made up, the Amazon returned to the control board and set course—one which would take them far out into space and then, in a gradual ellipse, bring them to approaching the leap-frog world from the rear. During this process, Abna stood and silently contemplated the stars; then presently he turned.

"I think there's one point we should get settled when we see Vashon," he said. "It might help us to decide whether or not Sazner really does belong to the leap-frog world. I mean the matter of radioactivity. We've discovered that Sazner is not affected by it. If Vashon and his race are not affected by it either, then I think we'll be entitled to assume that Sazner is definitely a member of the leap-frog world race—one of the Exodians, or whatever Vashon called them. On the other hand, if Vashon cannot stand radioactivity any more than we can, then we can suspect Sazner as being of another planet, possessing people of an entirely different basic makeup. Right?"

"Right," the Amazon agreed. "And the sooner we get to see Vashon, the better."

She turned back to the switches and began to put on the power, until presently the *Ultra* was hurtling through free space at an almost incredible pace.

"No sign of Sazner's machine anywhere," Mexone reported, after a careful astronomical survey. "Either he hasn't begun to return or else he's made the journey while we weren't on the watch."

"Either way we're going ahead," Abna answered briefly, and he crossed to the main observation window to survey.

It was evident, as the *Ultra* flew nearer, that the latest time-leap had been considerable—enough to change the entire pattern of the cone-like cities and the layout of the streets. Even the ground itself had changed color, indicating a considerable advance in years.

They left the *Ultra*—completely immobilized—and headed down the main street for Vashon's residence. As they went, people appeared in the streets adjoining the main one, and here and there vehicles came in sight. These vehicles were odd in outline, considerably advanced in design on any the travelers had seen previously.

"Things have certainly moved on," Abna commented, taking the lead up the palace steps. "Wonder if Vashon survived it?"

He had. They found him eventually in his own private suite, completely alone. He was seated at the curiously fashioned desk, and seemed to be in the midst of sorting out a pile of wafer-thin parchments. The moment the quartet came in upon him—unannounced, since there were apparently no guards on duty—his featureless head raised abruptly and looked in their direction. Immediately there came the vibration of his thoughts.

"Why, my friends! I had given you up for lost."

"Not quite," the Amazon responded. "Though none of us have any doubt that that was what Sazner intended. Has he returned yet from his cosmic investigations?"

"No—not yet." Vashon rose and began moving with a certain agitation. "He may be here at any moment, and you would be ill-advised to be present here when that happens."

"We'll chance it," Abna said grimly. "We don't pretend to be anything else but his enemies, and he knows it. Before he gets here, Vashon, we want one or two straight truths concerning him, and you're the only person who can tell us them. Are you prepared to co-operate?"

The ruler hesitated, apparently more from fear than anything else.

"What do you wish to know?"

"Many things," Abna responded. "In the first place, are you—or any members of your race—impervious to radioactivity?"

"Impervious to it? Why, certainly not! No living organism is that."

"Sazner is," the Amazon stated coldly, and the reaction on Vashon could be instantly sensed.

"But that isn't possible!" Vashon protested. "He is one of the Exodians from the north and they, like everybody else, are affected immediately by radioactivity."

The quartet looked significantly at one another. Then Abna posed another question.

"How often have you been to Sazner's laboratories, Excellency?"

"I haven't been at all. Sazner guards everything most jealously and permits no outsiders—not even me—to inspect the machines and instruments with which he creates the city's power. Indeed, not only for this city, but for most of the planet. It would not be good policy for me to be insistent on invading his scientific domain, particularly since I am not a very good scientist myself, so I do not say anything. I just accept and ask no questions."

"Which makes it just perfect for Sazner," Abna snapped.

"I don't understand you, my friend."

"I'll make it plainer. All your power is generated from the atom, which inevitably means immense radioactivity. The laboratory Sazner showed us is full of it, so much so that we said we'd need protective clothing. Sazner's answer to that was that it did not affect him, or any of the race."

"But that's utterly wrong!" Vashon protested.

"No doubt—and possibly Sazner said it without realizing it. But the damage was done then. Sazner, Excellency, is no more a member of this race of yours, or an Exodian, than we are. He is an alien, working deliberately against you—an alien who has a physical resemblance to you, but is basically entirely different from you. He apparently is helping you and the planet, but that is obviously only a blind. These so-called cosmic examinations he makes in space every time there is a time-leap can be classed as an excuse to make himself absent when a time-leap occurs. The reason for the absence is so he can make the time-leap possible by operating scientific equipment from a neighbor planet."

"But—but why should he wish to?" Vashon was plainly bewildered. "What's the purpose of it?"

"That we don't know yet, but we'll remain around here until we find out."

"We might take a short cut to that," the Amazon said. "Tell us, Excellency, what are the basic ingredients of this planet of yours? What is it made of?"

"Why—er—rock, soil, mineral substances—"

"What mineral substances?" the Amazon insisted.

The ruler made a vague motion of his tentacles, a sure enough sign that he did not know the answer.

"We can find out," Abna said. "Even without doing that I'll gamble that most of the substances are those which become radioactive as they advance in age. So, the farther time is advanced, the more radioactivity there is. We'll check on it—and the neighbor worlds, too. There's no longer any doubt in our minds, Excellency, but what Sazner is a member of a neighbor race that is determined to advance this planet of yours to a stage where it is highly radioactive."

"And destroy all of us on this world?" Vashon demanded. "That is, those that survive the time-leaps?"

"By the time the ultimate purpose is reached, I fancy everybody will be extinct anyway...." Abna mused for a moment; then: "I am a little puzzled as to why Sazner preserves you and a few high-ups each time. I can only think it is part of his scheme to let you think he's working for you instead of against you. You're in grave danger, Vashon—and so is everybody else on this planet. We assume the responsibility for straightening things out."

"All these revelations are most distressing, my friends. I would not say that I like Sazner as an individual, but I assumed his coldly dominant manner to be the outcome of his knowledge. I have never pictured him as an enemy."

"Then you can start picturing him as that from now on," the Amazon said curtly. "Why do you suppose he tried to wipe us out with chlorine gas? Why do you suppose he tried to crash us on the farthermost planet of the system? Because he's afraid of us! He knows we are scientists as good as himself, and as long as we survive, his own plans are in jeopardy—"

"He's coming back!" Mexone cut in abruptly, gazing at the window. "I just saw a small space machine touching down."

"Better move," Viona added urgently, with a half stride to the door.

"We'll move when we're disposed to," Abna decided, unshaken. "In any case, the fact that we're still alive has been betrayed by now by the very reason that the *Ultra*'s standing just outside the city."

"What do you propose to do when Sazner gets here?" Viona questioned, and at that Abna gave a grim smile.

"Try to get a few facts from him if I can. Straight facts, so we know what we're driving at—"

He broke off and tensed for action as the big door suddenly opened. There was a long pause as Sazner stood on the threshold appraising the situation. At least that was what he appeared to be doing. The slow side-to-side movement of his tulip-like head was the only indication. Then he abruptly turned about and returned into the main corridor. When he reappeared again he had four guards with him—pale green beings with weapons in their tentaculate hands.

"I absolutely forbid any violence," came the thought vibrations of Vashon, but there was an obvious timidity in his order.

"Naturally, Excellency, I am acting entirely in your interests," Sazner responded, coming forward and leaving the guards at the door. "It is no surprise to me to discover that these four aliens are still alive: their spaceship told me as much. It would appear that they are more difficult to exterminate than I had imagined."

"It is not my wish that they should be destroyed!" Vashon snapped.

"Apparently, Excellency, these four have endeavored to hoodwink you, even as at first they hoodwinked me. You do not seem to realize that they are deadly enemies of this world."

"You mean *you* are!" Abna put in coldly, and at that Sazner turned to him.

"I mean nothing of the kind. I am using every scientific trick I know to smash up your plans. I've known for long enough that the time-leaps peculiar to this planet have been created by scientists—that they are not a natural occurrence, but it never occurred to me that the perpetrators of this scientific outrage would come personally to view their handiwork."

For a second or two there was an impasse, then the Amazon sprang into sudden and violent life. So far she had been listening with growing fury to Sazner's observations—but as the full realization of his lies dawned upon her she reacted, as was natural to her, with lightning speed.

With one bound she had reached the queer being and seized him around the slender stem that she took to be his neck. To her surprise this was not a delicate organ: it had all the toughness of rubber hose. Evidently it was a vital spot, however, for Sazner made a frantic effort to save himself as the Amazon's steel-strong fingers tightened. In so doing he fell over backwards and remained pinned to the floor with the Amazon on top of him.

It all happened so swiftly that nobody else moved for a moment; then the guards in the doorway jerked up their weapons in readiness to settle the issue—only they never even started. In one flying bound Abna was across the room, taking on two guards at once. The first one he sent spinning from a terrific blow in the face—or what there was of it. The second one he picked up bodily, whirled him over his head with his immense strength, and then threw him a distance of a dozen yards. Once he hit the wall and slithered to the floor, the guard did not rise again.

The remaining two stood no chance either. Viona dealt with one, battering him down with her fists until he lay gasping on the floor; and the second one fell to the uppercuts of Mexone. In a matter of three minutes each guard was completely out of action, the trio ready to strike with devastating force for the second time if need be.

"Quite like old times," Abna grinned, glancing at the Amazon. "Carry on with whatever you intend doing."

She nodded, her fingers still gripping the helpless Sazner's throat. Vashon looked on in wonder, unaccustomed to such a display of superhuman strength.

"There are times," the Amazon said, addressing the squirming scientist beneath her, "when all normal approaches are of no avail. You've consistently lied to his Excellency concerning us, Sazner, so perhaps a little physical violence will make you tell the truth."

Another blow, and yet another, brought Sazner so close to collapse that he apparently hardly knew what he was doing. His speech was chaotic; his thoughts confused.

"Yes—yes, I am doing it. I have done it. I am controlling basic forces of Time and Space...."

"How?" the Amazon snapped. "What method do you use?"

"Control of probability laws. Shift and change bound up in the atom. Change the time course of the atom and you change the time course of any form of matter. Time and space are linked. You cannot...you cannot move one without the other."

Sazner's voice had been sinking as he had been talking. Now it ceased entirely and his thoughts blanked out. For a moment or two the Amazon kept her hold upon him, musing over what he had said and the tremendous scientific implications contained therein— then she relaxed slightly—and thereby learned the truth of the statement that one should never turn one's back on the enemy.

Sazner came to life again, with tremendous energy and fury gathered from his short respite. Before she realized what had happened, the Amazon found herself pitched away on to the floor. Neither she, Abna, Mexone, nor Viona had a chance to act before Sazner had whipped one of the guards' weapons from the floor and leveled it.

"Now, my friends...." Sazner got slowly to his feet, his thoughts filled with cold triumph. "Now let us assess the situation properly. What I told you just now was, of course, sheer nonsense. I cannot move Time: that is left to such scientists as you, scientists full of vicious intrigue who are determined to destroy this planet. You hear me, Excellency?"

"I hear you," Vashon assented, uncertain.

"To save everything I have only one course," Sazner continued. "I have to destroy these four. I have tried twice by elaborate scientific methods. Possibly a better result can be obtained by the simple use of this gun."

CHAPTER SIX
RADIOACTIVE REVELATIONS

For a second or two there was a grim pause. The Amazon, who by now was on her feet again, was nearest to Sazner. She eyed him and the gun narrowly—then with that speed which was her main characteristic, she catapulted herself forward in a flying tackle. Sazner's weapon stabbed a jet of fire even as she grabbed him around the lower part of his ridiculous body and brought him down.

"Get out!" she shouted hoarsely, slamming her fists into the flower-like head. "I'll follow."

"'Finish him off and save a lot of trouble!" Viona insisted.

"Not until we've got more information from him," the Amazon retorted. "It's useless right now: too many things are against us. Do as you're told and get out."

A final smashing downward blow on Sazner's head completely stunned him. Only then did the Amazon rise. She glanced toward the door, toward which Abna, Mexone, and Viona were already. hurrying, and then she turned to the ruler.

"Things are too difficult for us to stay here, Vashon,"

she explained quickly. "We have a great deal to do. I cannot make you believe that we are fighting for you, but that is the solemn truth. Sazner is your enemy, not us. We'll return later when we have the situation under better control than it is now."

Vashon did not respond. He was plainly trying to fathom the situation. The Amazon stayed no longer, but raced out of the great room in pursuit of the other three. She caught up with them as they were about to enter the *Ultra*.

"You're still sure it wouldn't be a better idea to finish Sazner while we have the chance?" Abna demanded, hesitating.

"Only a fool is sure of anything, Abna—but I do realize that we have only touched the fringe of Sazner's scientific scheming as yet. We may need him for further elaboration of that theory he explained about time and space. He's tampering with the Law of Probability, and if he's dead, we may not get certain vital facts that are necessary. Leave him be for now: we have other work to do."

Abna said no more. He led the way through the open airlock, the others coming behind him. In a matter of three minutes the airlock was shut and the huge machine was streaking through the atmosphere towards outer space. Once the void was gained, the Amazon relaxed slightly and switched in the automatic pilot. Then she turned to where Abna, Viona, and Mexonc were regarding her in silent inquiry.

"I still think Sazner should have been finished off,"

Viona muttered. "And that isn't because I'm blood-thirsty."

"No, just thoughtless," the Amazon said dryly. "I have already explained to your father that Sazner may be useful to us yet, and on top of that there is the possibility that he is not the only one in this scheme. His decease would only mean his replacement by somebody else. When we're ready, we'll deal with him effectually enough."

"And in the meanwhile?" Mexone inquired.

"Meanwhile, I think we should make a study of each planet in this system and see if we can discover what advantage Sazner hopes to gain by advancing one of them in Time. Might as well get on that job right away," the Amazon finished, and with that she crossed to the analyzing equipment and set it in action. The final readings were interesting.

The outermost world, planet of monsters, showed a very low radioactive reading. On the other hand, the leap-frog planet had an extremely high radioactive reading. Another of the worlds, the one towards which Sazner's ship had been seen heading—and where it was suspected Sazncr had originated and probably had his scientific apparatus—had a medium radioactivity in a state of extreme fluctuation. The basis of the planet itself appeared to be lead. The remaining planets revealed no radioactive reading of any significance.

"Any suggestions?" Abna asked, as he studied the reports. "Can you see any clue in these as to why the time-leaps are created?"

"Yes, I think so," the Amazon responded, surprisingly. "In the first place, Sazner's planet—if it really is that—is a good deal older than all the other worlds. Once it was probably highly radioactive. Now it is mainly lead, which in some cases is the last material condition of a radioactive substance. In other words, the fires of its radioactivity have burned low. We know that Sazner is not affected by radioactivity. I'll go one further and say that it is a vital necessity to him and his race, if they are to continue living. Agreed?"

"Very possible," Abna assented. "So?"

"So, probably facing destruction on their own planet through the death of radioactivity, they are preparing Vashon's planet in this elaborate way to the moment when they can take it over. The readings already show high radioactivity. Another two leaps, perhaps, and maximum could be reached. After that will begin the slow deterioration over tens of thousands of years."

Abna rubbed his chin slowly. "Certainly has the ring of possibility about it, Vi," he admitted at length, "but of all the ways to get a planet to live on, it's the most amazing one yet! Apparently, though, his system isn't absolutely perfect, otherwise there would not be survivors each time. There always seem to be some men and women—if you can call those tulip objects that—who escape."

"Why," Viona asked, puzzled, "is Vashon and those next to him allowed to escape every time? Surely, from Sazner's point of view, they'd be better out of the way?"

"Probably...." The Amazon gave a grim smile "But Sazner is a clever man: he always looks two steps ahead. He knows that if Vashon and his important retinue were to be wiped out, his scientific prowess would be questioned by other important personalities on the planet. Don't forget he's supposed to be a savior, not a destroyer. If he permitted the deaths of the high-ups, he might be questioned too closely for his liking."

"Then it simply resolves into one issue," Abna said, in the quietness. "We must go to Sazner's world and destroy him, his people, and everything connected with him."

The Amazon did not reply. Her brows knitted and, pondering something to herself, she, too, moved to the big window and surveyed. Abna followed her up, plainly surprised that she had not responded to his statement.

"I'm right, am I not?" he asked presently.

"Oh, yes—very right. But we're at the toughest part of the whole campaign. In the first place, Sazner will never for a moment be caught off guard. He'll watch for us constantly, and where he cannot do so, he'll certainly have others do it for him. In the second place, if we could even approach his planet without being detected—which I doubt—we don't know the exact spot where the devilment is centralized, and for us to attack anything less than the heart would be a prodigious risk and waste of time.... Somehow," the Amazon finished, beating her tawny fist gently on the window ledge, "we have to locate the exact spot without giving ourselves away. I frankly admit that I don't know how."

"In some things," Abna smiled, "you are completely lost. Metaphysics, for example; and that's the answer to our present problem."

"Meaning what?"

Abna glanced at the instruments. "At the moment we're far enough to the edge of this System to be out of range of anything Sazner might train upon us—or, more simply, he doesn't know whether we are near at hand or gone for good. There's only one way to follow him now and see his exact hideout, and that is by linking my mind to his."

"I see." The Amazon did not look pleased; but then she never did when Abna worked in fields beyond her understanding.

"But, Dad, granting you can do that," Viona said, coming forward, "is it such a good idea? Don't forget Sazner is a telepath. Instead of you reading his thoughts, he may read yours and from that locate where we are."

Abna smiled. "This isn't a case of thought-reading. It's mental projection. I've done it on one or two occasions before, as you know, but the effort is so severe I don't attempt it often. It simply means that my mind sees through the mind of Sazner. For the time being I become a kind of ghost of him, seeing through his eyes, ears, and general senses—wherever he keeps them in such a queer body. That way I should be able to find out all we want to know."

"Which we can't do until he sets off for his planet from Vashon's world," Mexone pointed out, and Abna nodded.

"The moment there is a reaction, cut the radar off," Abna instructed. "We don't want to give Sazner the remotest chance of detecting anything."

Viona nodded but passed no comment.

"I just wonder what he's up to?" the Amazon muttered, visibly chafing at the inaction. "Can't be anything good, whatever it is."

Abna shrugged. "Probably making his peace with Vashon and incriminating us as much as possible at the same time. It may be many days, or even weeks, before he decides to move on—"

"No it won't," came Viona's quick voice. "He's on his way now—or at any rate something is. Take a look."

Immediately Abna and the Amazon were at her side, gazing intently at the radar screen. There was no doubt about the small spot of light moving away from the semi-circular blur which represented the edge of Vashon's planet. It soon became evident that he was headed for the neighbor world they had seen him approaching earlier, before they had been flung through space to the monster planet.

"That's Sazner, all right," Abna said promptly. "If it isn't, I shall very soon know once I've contacted his mind. Shut that thing off, Viona—and don't any of you interrupt me from here on."

There was silence, each one knowing the concentrated effort into which Abna was now about to plunge. He crossed to the nearest wall couch, lay flat upon it, and closed his eyes. To him, after a little preliminary mental probing, it was then as though he had gradually assumed the senses of Sazner himself, but none of his personal emotions. He saw through his eyes—or at any rate the organs that passed therefore—and heard through his ears. He was seated in the small control cabin of the little space machine, gazing out on to the endless void.

Then the planet loomed into view, grew steadily larger as Sazner's ship approached it. Far ahead, as Abna 'watched' through Sazner, something like a valve began to open, very much like a monstrous eye. The space machine went through the opening and thereafter began to descend into a brilliantly lighted underworld. Here, as Abna quickly noticed, there were hundreds of tulip creatures at work, like termites in some gigantic mechanized anthill. There was no time for Abna to observe the immense machines at close quarters, for the space machine flashed past them, until it at last came to rest somewhere in the center of them. At this point his own resources compelled him to break contact.

He stirred slowly and opened his eyes. The anxiously waiting faces of the Amazon, Viona, and Mexone were looking down upon him.

"Well?" the Amazon demanded. "Did you discover anything?"

Abna struggled up from the wall couch and sat meditating for a moment; then he gave his curiously boyish grin.

"Discover anything? I discovered the lot—even

to how our flower-like friend enters his world. It's a planet with an underground civilization, entirely given over—far as I could tell—to scientific machinery."

"Mmmm, that's logical," the Amazon reflected. "On a world which is nearly dead, as the analyzer showed, the inhabitants would naturally take to the underworld to lessen the rigors and conserve their own natural resources.... But what's the situation for us? How do we get into this world?"

"Sazner does it by entering a single valve—which can't possibly be missed in such a barren landscape, but whether the valve would open for us as it did for him is questionable, unless it operates by some kind of photoelectric system, which means that any object crossing the beam will open the valve."

"Sounds risky," Mexone commented, with a dubious glance.

"There's only one possibility," the Amazon decided. "We must make the *Ultra* invisible and explore over this valve to see if it will open. If it doesn't by photoelectric means, we'll perhaps take a chance and blast it open. Agreed?"

There was no hesitation. The course was a risky one, but to the Crusaders risks were as natural as breathing. So, satisfied that the others were willing, the Amazon wasted no more time. She turned to the switchboard and, by degrees, the aspect of the *Ultra* gradually changed. The immensely thick walls appeared to slowly dissolve until they were apparently no longer there. The stars blazed through the darkness, and an unshielded sun poured out its saturating radiance. Actually, no miracle had been accomplished, unless it was one of supreme science. Energy had so thinned the material construction of the *Ultra*'s hull that it had become as transparent as glass. It was the nearest thing to invisibility, since the darkness of space was all an observer could see through this transparency. True, the power plant and other equipment were still solid, as were the travelers themselves, but to spot these alone floating in the void would require telescopic excellence indeed.

So the journey continued steadily, and from a pinprick in the infinite distance Sazner's world grew to a planet of sizeable dimensions. The closer it came the more obvious was its burned-out, sun-saturated surface. That it was a world on the edge of doom was more than obvious.

"Okay," the Amazon said finally, rising from the switch-panel seat. "You'd better take over from here, Abna, since you know the terrain in advance."

He nodded and took the Amazon's place. The *Ultra* had not arrived on this world at the same point as Sazner's machine had done, so Abna simply kept the *Ultra* going forward at 1,000 miles an hour 100 miles up in the thin air, and meanwhile kept a close watch on the pumice-like landscape below.

Everything he had seen through the senses of Sazner had registered photographically on his mind, so when at length he came over a familiar region, he knew exactly where he was and began to tilt the *Ultra*'s nose downwards.

The valve was looming ahead in the landscape, exactly like an eye as its cover slid ponderously to one side. Abna turned the *Ultra* slightly and headed straight for it.

"You're going below, then?" the Amazon asked, giving him a brief glance.

"Certainly I am. Nothing to be gained flying round and round the surface. We'll take whatever comes."

Even as he had been speaking the *Ultra* had reached the opening. It flashed through it and then commenced to cruise leisurely high above the vast machine-city housed in the depths of the planet, and evidently illuminated by some unseen artificial source that gave the effect of full daylight in the underworld.

To Abna, who had already seen it all through the medium of Sazner, there was nothing new or novel about it—but for the Amazon, Viona, and Mexone it had a fascination all its own.

"Here," the Amazon said presently, in obvious admiration, "we have a people who have perfected science to the ultimate degree, no matter how queer their physical vestment may be.... We haven't an easy job on our hands, Abna."

"I never believed that we had...." Abna was busy swinging the near-invisible machine downwards to the central point where he had seen Sazner land his own vessel. How correct his judgment was, was revealed presently as Sazner's spaceship came into view in the central square. Although he knew full well the risk he was taking, Abna kept on going, finally bringing the *Ultra* down to gentle rest. It seemed to him as he switched off the power plant that the humming of the energy converters ceased with unusual abruptness. The Amazon noticed it, too, and gave a sharp glance.

"I didn't quite like the sound of that...." She came over quickly. "The power died a second or two before you cut it off—or sounded to."

Abna stood in silence as she switched the power on again—or at least that was what she intended to do. Nothing happened, however. The switches were dead—and not only those controlling the power plant, but all the others as well. Now it came to be observed, it was obvious that the emergency battery lighting had imperceptibly taken over from the normal circuit.

"Dead," the Amazon muttered, glancing about her. "Our power has been cut off.... Not," she finished grimly, "that it is anything more than I really expected."

"A little problem like neutralizing our power would hardly puzzle scientists as clever as these," Abna commented, shrugging. "Don't forget they were able to create a warp in space and fling us away when we tried to follow Sazner earlier.... But at least we still have our guns, and those can do plenty of damage if need be—"

He broke off as it suddenly sounded as though a voice spoke from somewhere. After a second or two it became apparent that it was not actual speech as much as heavily amplified telepathic vibration.

"It would be better, my friends, if your insatiable curiosity were satisfied by a closer examination of the city in which you find yourselves. Open your airlock, and after that follow the directions which will be given you."

"Better do as he says," Ahna said finally, then as the Amazon seemed about to flare into bitter comment, he gave her a warning look. It was obvious that Sazner could see and hear them, so there was no sense in giving away more than was necessary.

Once they were outside the vessel and surrounded by the vast machines, which seemed to take the place of normal city buildings, the four forgot a good deal of their personal fears in their interest.

There were also transformers, turbine-like objects, anode and cathode globes, and indeed the whole gamut of an electrical wilderness. Everything was linked together by aisles or bridges. On the latter were countless flower people, moving silently about their engineering tasks, taking not the least notice of the four travelers who passed slowly below them in open wonder. In regard to the flower-people themselves, the one outstanding thing about them was their scarlet color, exactly similar to Sazner's own. Here, plainly, was a race quite apart from anything produced on the world of Vashon.

Presently, still moving under directions, the quartet left the main aisle and, following a short gangway, they came at length to a region where the huge machines had been replaced by dwellings, most of them of the same cone-shape as those on the world of Vashon. The central one, larger than the rest, was apparently the ultimate destination, since it was to here that the four found themselves led.

They entered, walked down a long corridor, and so at length found themselves opening a door that gave on to a long, low-ceilinged room. At the far end was a curiously shaped desk, and behind it one of the strange curled chairs exclusively used by these odd people.

That the being at the desk was Sazner there was no doubt. He remained motionless, his tentacle hands slightly raised above a row of switches to either side of him. When the four had gained the desk, a push on a button caused locks to click across the main doors to the rear. Other things happened, too, which the four could not detect even though they could hear sounds. They strongly suspected—rightly, as it happened—that weapons had become uncovered somewhere and were trained on them.

"Very persistent, are you not?" Sazner's thoughts asked coldly. "Having already escaped my two efforts to destroy you, you are still prying into matters which are not your concern.... I think your persistency should be rewarded."

"In what way?" Abna demanded.

"Well, apparently you have hit on the truth—that I am advancing the neighbor world in time for my own ends; so for having been so observant you are entitled to some kind of recompense, nothing less than the actual experience of traveling through time and space. You see, my friends, there is much that you have to learn in the matter of controlling the atom...."

"Oh?" the Amazon asked cynically.

"I once said—under pressure—that Time was bound up in the law of probability. That was correct. We have always to remember that the fact that Time is now can change to the equally important factor that Time is past or future. There is nothing stable about Time. Because in the vast majority of cases the atom governing the condition remains constant, we are apt to assume that Time is a steady, permanent thing. This is not so. Produce enough power to shift the atom into another plane entirely, and we have a corresponding advancement or retrogression through Time."

"Surely that implies absolute control of the atom?" the Amazon inquired. "The normal consequences of shifting the atomic plane is to bring about a tremendous explosion."

"Yes, because all atoms are not moved at once. In this case the entire set-up is changed without a single atom being left out. That, visibly, means that matter itself changes, since the atom is the basis of matter. It is only possible to do this in stages, since the amount of energy needed to involve every atom in a planet is prodigious."

"The planet being the world of Vashon?" Abna asked.

"Exactly. We could do it with any planet, but that happens to be the one we're interested in. It has already made several leaps forward in Time, and before long our ultimate objective will have been reached."

"Which is a world of radioactivity, so that you and

your race can survive," the Amazon said coldly. "Your own world is now becoming deficient in this respect, so you must have a planet which is rich in it. In order to achieve this end, you ruthlessly advance Vashon's world in Time, caring nothing for the destruction of his race, just as long as it suits you and your fellows."

"It is the ageless struggle to survive," Sazner said calmly.

"No, I don't think it is." The Amazon shook her head vigorously. "Your world, by the natural order of things, is a good deal older than the other planets. It has borne life upon it for a chosen period, and you should be content to die with your world and give the other planets and the peoples upon them a chance. But, your science is such that you can force your will upon other worlds, and obviously intend to do so. Being an older race than the others, you have naturally learned more—and you are intending to use that knowledge to your own ends.... But it won't succeed, Sazner. It might have done, but you have four here who are your equal, and even your superior. We are dedicated to the protection of Vashon and his people."

"You talk like a fool. I admit your ingenuity, but even that has its limits."

The Amazon's hand tightened on the butt of her gun.

CHAPTER SEVEN
PRIMEVAL WORLD

"Obviously," Sazner said, rising from his desk, "you are in need of a practical demonstration. Do you imagine that Time can only move futurewards, or that it can only apply to Vashon's world? For instance...."

A tentacle moved and touched one of the buttons. Instantly the Amazon pulled forth her gun, but she hesitated to fire it. That slight hesitation proved fatal, for the next instant she was frozen into immobility. Out of the corner of her eye she could see that Abna, Viona, and Mexone were likewise held rigid. It was an old but extremely effective method of pinning an enemy.

"Now," Sazner observed, "we shall see how much good you can do for Vashon and his race.... I believe that the most valuable asset you have is your space machine, the *Ultra*. Without it—if I have read your minds correctly—you are unable to return home."

The Amazon made a desperate mental and physical effort to break the iron paralysis that held her, but without avail. Even Abna seemed quite unable to break the spell.

"You shall now see a practical demonstration of

time travel," Sazner continued. "And just in case you have any ideas about escape, we will make sure of that now."

In response to his signal a dozen or so flower beings came forward from an adjoining room. Clearly they were guards—or something very similar. They took each member of the party, two to each person, and lifted them rigid and horizontal above their queer, flower-like heads. In this wise the quartet was transported to one of the countless machine-rooms, and presently set down on their feet once more. Still helpless, the four waited for Sazner to catch up, which presently he did.

"I will allow you to retain your weapons," he said, "for the simple reason that you will probably have good reason to use them.... You have already seen a world that is young in evolution—populated by monsters and the beasts of pre-civilized times—but did you ever pause to think what might exist before that?"

Abruptly they were falling—or at least that was the impression conveyed. They seemed to be tumbling down an enormous and totally dark shaft. It was so sudden, it caught them completely by surprise. They had barely time to grasp the new circumstances in which they found themselves before the paralysis ceased and they were capable of movement,

Each of them was lying on his or her back, gazing up at a gray and unfriendly sky. Of laboratory, of Sazner, there was no trace. They were somewhere in past Time, and by all the laws of logic, had not yet even been created. Slowly, uncertainly, the Amazon sat up and looked about her. Abna did likewise. Then after a moment or so, Mexone and Viona followed suit.

The view was limited. Overhead was the gray unformed sky, a mass of slow-moving clouds, while, down at ground level the view was uninspiring, because of mist. It encompassed perhaps 100 yards on every side, and that was all. The main impression was of being on a rocky landscape, desolate and alone, with no sign of a living thing.

"Well," the Amazon commented at length, standing up, "I don't see anything particularly terrifying about this. The most disturbing factor is that we are without the *Ultra*—and without that there is hardly a thing we can do."

Abna did not answer. He was looking about him thoughtfully—up at the leaden sky, at the all-surrounding mist. And he seemed, too, to be listening intently.

"I believe," he said at last, "that I can hear something."

The others were quiet, staring about them in the mist. Then after a while they heard the sound that had attracted Abna. It was a queer clicking note, rather like muted castanets, and was growing in intensity from all sides.

"I don't know what it is," the Amazon said finally, "but I certainly don't like it."

She yanked out her proton gun and took a step forward, only to hesitate as something emerged out of the mist. It looked like a tree branch and shot over her head at lightning speed.

"Do you see what they are?" Mexone cried, his voice half way between amazement and revulsion. "They're bacteria! Enormously magnified!"

"You're right!" the Amazon agreed after a moment. "The most indestructible form of life there is. They can survive both boiling water and the absolute zero of space—" She dodged as one came hurtling dangerously close. "But what are they doing at the beginning of evolution? I could well understand them being at the end, as the last survivors, but to be at the commencement of life is a mystery to me—"

"We've got to move," Abna said grimly. "This lot will wear us down it we don't—I don't know what's in the mist, but it surely can't be worse than this. Come on!"

To look at it, the forest was more or less normal—until one came to advance. Then the quartet found danger at every step. Apparent tendrils turned out to be thin, venomous snakes, which only a lightning movement of the proton gun destroyed. Giant puffballs uncoiled to reveal something that was a cross between a gigantic spider and a hedgehog, hanging on a strand of web as thick as a man's arm. Even the trees themselves had some reflex action, and leaned menacingly as the bewildered four passed by them. Just in time they saw branches and deadly sucker leaves reaching toward them and dodged quickly out of the way.

So at length they came to a clearer stretch in the formidable forest—a region where natural grass was waist-high and where fantastic life did not appear quite so prolific.

"Seems to me," the Amazon said, looking around her, "that either the upper regions of these trees are very dense, or else night is coming."

Abna looked above. The sky was hardly visible, so dense was the foliage, but what little he could see was dimming from grayness to blackness. Evidently the planet had a rapid revolution, which meant night would fall with extreme swiftness.

"You're right," he replied. "We'd better make this spot our base camp for the night and then decide tomorrow what we are going to do."

By the time they had finished a shelter—a roughly contrived affair with four corner props supporting a mass of leaves—it was totally dark.

Viona lighted a fire, and in the fitful glow the four looked at each other, feeling more lost than they had ever done in their adventurous lives.

"I suppose," the Amazon said at length, sighing, "I hardly need to emphasize our difficulties. We've no food or water, and if starvation or thirst doesn't kill us, the forest certainly will. I've been doing plenty of thinking ever since we got pushed back in time, but I can't find a solution."

"There surely ought to be something to eat on this planet," Mexone insisted. "Even if it's only fruit. With those pangs satisfied, we might be able to think more clearly. First things first."

"He's right," Abna decided, rising to his feet. "I

think the best thing we can do, Vi, is search for food. You and Viona can either stay here or come with us."

The Amazon rose also and tested the torch from her belt. The small atomic battery—with a life of hundreds of years—gave forth an eerie circle of light into the surrounding dark.

"We'll all search," she decided. "The fire will act as a guide back to our base camp here. Let's go."

Suddenly, unexpectedly, they came upon a pond. It was perhaps fifty feet across, its surface slimed with green algae. In silence they stood looking at it, each wondering if it were water fit to drink.

"I hardly think it is," Abna said finally, interpreting all their thoughts. "Too much stagnation about it."

He went closer, squatting down at the water's edge, and stirring it up with a piece of stick. As the brilliant gleam of his torch penetrated into the depths he gave a start. Something swam momentarily into the light, and then was gone. Soon it was followed by another, and still another. At first he mistook them for fish, then as one moved more slowly than the others—not unlike a shapeless mass of jelly—he looked up in surprise.

"Recognize what those things are?" he asked, as the Amazon, Viona and Mexone gazed with him.

"Some kind of water life," the Amazon said, disappointedly. "No use to us—"

"They're more than water life." Abna's voice was deeply thoughtful. "They're amoeba!"

"Which doesn't get us any nearer any food," the Amazon said irritably, and she went on her way around the edge of the pond. Indeed, she had penetrated some distance into the forest with Viona and Mexone behind her, before it occurred to her that Abna was not with them.

Turning, she flashed her torch beam back along the blazed trail they had followed. At that moment Abna came into view, a look of profound concentration on his face.

"We thought we'd lost you," the Amazon told him. "Where have you been?"

"Nowhere. Just pondering beside the lake. I've got an idea, Vi. A possible way to defeat Sazner which he would certainly never think of, otherwise he wouldn't have sent us here. In fact, not only him, but his whole race."

"Oh?" The Amazon waited for him to continue, then before he could do so there was a sudden interruption from Mexone.

"Look at these! If they're edible—"

He hurried forward, the torchlight dancing on a tree, which stood in isolation from the others. What was important about it was that it was heavy with melon-like fruits.

The Amazon, Abna, and Viona came over to him quickly, and each stood surveying the tree hungrily.

Finally Abna strode forward, pulled down one of the fruits, and examined it critically in torchlight.

"Looks all right," he said finally. "And I suppose there is only one sure way to tell."

So saying he took a deep bite of the fruit, chewed

experimentally, and then swallowed. In anxious silence the others waited, but minute succeeded minute and finally Abna grinned widely.

"Evidently my number isn't in the frame yet," he commented. "I'd say they're harmless. Get busy and try some."

There and then a meal was made of the fruits, and as many as could he carried were taken down. It still left hundreds more for future use.

"Granting there are no ill-effects, that's our food and drink problem solved," the Amazon said. "The juice from them is a drink in itself."

Abna did not answer. He was exploring the ground beneath the tree, and for that matter in various directions. Here and there he picked up a handful of the queer, dry soil and inspected it carefully. Finally he tested some in his pocket analyzer.

"Queer," he pronounced, half to himself. "Very queer."

"What is?" The Amazon, laden with melons, looked at him curiously.

"The soil around here—in fact, everywhere. It's not soil in the sense that we understand it. It's made up of fissionable materials."

The Amazon reflected for a moment. "Well, is that so very odd? Don't forget that we made a reading of this planet in its normal Time and it was radioactive. That makes fissionable material quite normal."

"True, but—" Abna stood up slowly and pondered again. "It can also mean something else—something that ties up with the amoeba in the pond."

"I wish you'd stop talking in riddles," the Amazon objected. "Think it out carefully and then let's hear it. In the meantime, grab as many fruits as you can and let's get back to base."

Abna did as he was told, entirely absently. He was still lost in thought when eventually the shelter had been regained and the 'melons' had been stacked for future use.

Viona and Mexone immediately fell to some muttered conversation in the background, while the Amazon rekindled the fire. She had just finished this task when a thought seemed to strike her.

"Abna...." She came over to where he was sitting brooding.

"Well?"

"Would fruit grown in fissionable ground be poisonous? I mean, that tree is growing in that sort of soil, and it seems to me that if—"

"If there were to be any ill-effects, we'd have detected them by now," Abna answered. "Fissionable doesn't mean radioactive; it means capable of *becoming* radioactive, and that is what is so intriguing me."

"But why?" The Amazon sat down beside him. "Tell me more."

Abna knitted his brows. "I can't altogether get it into clear focus, but it seems to me that we have in our hands the power to destroy all Sazner's race, and him with it. They would vanish as though they had never been, and with them would go all danger to Vashon's world."

His words brought Viona and Mexone from the back of the shelter. They squatted nearby and listened.

"We're agreed, I suppose, that life begins with the amoeba," Abna went on. "That each amoeba is responsible for what later becomes a living being? Let's put it more simply. Assume that this is Earth, teeming with its millions of human beings. Each of those human beings sprang from the amoeba, to begin with."

"Yes," the Amazon assented. "But I don't see what you are getting at."

"Just this. The amoeba we have seen, and, of course, the amoeba which must exist in various parts of this planet—mostly in the ponds, since that is where amoeba are mainly found—are the basis of the race from which Sazner has sprung. Without the amoeba, there could be no race."

"Oh—yes," said the Amazon. "Destroy the amoeba and you destroy the race. While the amoeba exist, the flower men exist, too, because the chain of evolution is unbroken. But destroy the amoeba and the course of evolution is changed—it ceases to exist. Sazner and his race will disappear."

"Just so," Abna agreed, musing. "Come to think of it, it may well be that certain races on Earth which have mysteriously disappeared, leaving all their achievements behind them, have been obliterated by some such occurrence in past Time. Anyway, be that as it may, our concern is the amoeba on this world." He paused for a moment, then said deliberately: "Every amoeba on this planet has got to be eliminated."

"But that's impossible," the Amazon objected. "There must be tens of millions of them spawning in the ponds and oceans. To destroy them is utterly impossible. It—it would take a fire or something of planet-sized proportions to do it. I know it would theoretically destroy Sazner and his race, but it just can't be done."

Abna smiled gravely. "That is where the fissionable material comes in."

The Amazon's bewilderment was complete. "What has that got to do with it?"

"Everything. Yon agree that if we started an atomic chain-reaction it would spread around this planet like wildfire, destroying everything at ground level? The amoeba are at that level, and would perish in the boiling ponds, or else the raging fire which would sweep along the ground."

"I grant you the correctness of your theory," the Amazon sighed. "But it's just a pipe dream, Abna, incapable of achievement. For one thing, even if it could be done, what about us? We'd perish, too, in the chain reaction."

"The time in which we'd be involved in the holocaust would only be brief—thirty minutes at the most. I think each one of us has enough control of mind over matter to keep ourselves untouched for that period. It is a matter of metaphysical effort."

"You sound," Viona exclaimed in wonder, "as though you really mean to do it, father."

"Certainly I mean to do it." He glanced at her. "We

each have four guns between us. In them is a tremendous amount of energy if it were released at one time—but it is controlled. I suggest that we take out the copper plug which forms the basis of the atomic power, and then discharge all of it at once."

The Amazon knitted her brows. "It's a wonderful scheme, Abna, and one which I wouldn't have thought of myself. But I foresee certain difficulties. I think that all the metaphysical protection in the world will be insufficient to save the one that fires the gun. It will blow you to pieces the instant the copper releases its energy."

"We'll get over that by some system of remote control," Abna shrugged. "Maybe a vine, used as string, to pull the required part of the gun. That is the least of our difficulties."

"And at the end of it all," the Amazon said slowly. "What of us? Granting we even survive, we'll be left on a world that is stripped bare of everything. The bacteria will survive because they can take to the air. We shall be at their mercy—without guns, without anything. And we shall have destroyed all our food plants as well. We're just committing suicide."

"Perhaps....," Abna said, thinking.

"No perhaps about it. It's obvious!"

Abna seemed to reflect, then: "The fact remains that for the moment the most obvious course is to try to do what I have suggested. Give me your guns."

They were handed over. Very carefully he removed the main firing piece from each. Having got this far, he reached around until he found a length of vine. With this he proceeded to tie the four copper firing pieces into a bundle, lowering them finally into a hole scooped into the crumbly ground.

"We need only one gun to fire the stuff," he said, "and it might as well be mine."

The others took their weapons back and watched him anxiously in the firelight as he fastened the vine to the trigger mechanism of his own gun and tested it once or twice. Each time there was, as expected, a brilliant flash. Satisfied, Abna fixed the gun so that when it discharged it would strike directly on the four firing pieces—then he began to pay the vine out like a length of rope until he had reached the end. This placed him some twenty-five feet away from the atomic 'pile.'

"That's it," he said simply, as the Amazon glanced at him in the dimly reflected light of the fire. "Once I pull this vine, the stuff will be detonated and we'll have lighted the powder keg."

He waited until the Amazon, Viona, and Mexone were well to the rear of him. Then he took one last look around. A sudden thought seemed to strike him.

"Lie flat and cover your eyes. The flash will be intensely bright."

He waited until his instructions had been obeyed; then lying full length and covering his own eyes, he pulled the vine taut.

For an instant nothing happened. The copper absorbed the charge, and for a fraction of a second there was an interval as the release of energy took place.

Abna had expected it, and kept his eyes shielded.

It was as well he did so, for suddenly there burst forth from the bundle an unholy glare of light. It transformed the night into five times day, and almost as quickly died out again. There was no violent explosion, no anything except a sizzling noise like a white-hot poker thrust into cold water. Slowly Abna dared to look, and the others, too, raised their heads. In silence they lay watching.

The effort had succeeded. Around the vital area was a slowly growing black hole; its edges fringed with rippling flame as the chain reaction proceeded. Downwards and outwards the crater was expanding, destroying everything in its track.

"Do you still believe that the fissionable material only goes down for a certain distance?" the Amazon asked, studying the phenomenon.

Abna nodded. "I think it highly unlikely that it goes right through the planet. If so, the planet itself would be destroyed and that would mean that there couldn't have been a planet in the future. Since there is, I assume I am correct."

The logic was obvious. The Amazon stepped back a few paces as the line of flame made rapid advance in her direction. Finally she gave Abna a quick look.

"We're going to be forced back constantly by this line of fire, Abna. What's the answer? If we jump beyond it, we'll drop into a hole that's one mass of radioactivity."

"No reason why it should be," he replied. "The radioactivity is occurring along this line of flames; beyond it is dead and finished. The only point is we don't know how far down the crater goes. I'm going to take a leap and at the same time use metaphysical means to protect myself against injury. As you others follow me, I'll do my utmost to save you, too.... Here goes."

He went back several paces, then taking a running jump, he sailed well clear of the rim of creeping fire and landed in the dark gulf beyond. To the others it seemed that he utterly disappeared, whereas the truth was that he dropped a matter of fifteen or twenty feet and landed deep in the midst of ash and powder. To have called it the remains of fire would hardly have sufficed: the atomic destruction had wiped everything into the consistency of fine dust.

"Come on!" Abna yelled. "It's perfectly safe!"

There was a moment's pause, then a dark figure became apparent hurdling the sizzling rim at the top. In another moment the Amazon was knee-deep in the ashes. Turning, Abna helped her up.

He had hardly done so before Viona and Mexonc came flying through the air. They landed, struggled upwards, and then stood gazing at the glowing edge of the crater as it expanded away from them.

"Now what?" the Amazon asked. "Stop here indefinitely, without food or water?"

Abna shook his head. "I was prepared for this, and I think there is a way out."

CHAPTER EIGHT
INTO FUTURITY

For a moment or two there was silence, except for the steady hiss of disintegration from the atomic line of fire. Already it was fast receding, leaving the quartet in this blackened crater from which all life had gone.

Abna said: "During our battles with Sefner Quorne, there was once a time when we used mental means to transfer ourselves from one part of the universe to another. In that case the factor of space was involved: in this instance it is the factor of Time, not space, since we have moved very little since our original arrival here.... All Sazner did was shift our probability units, and the fact that we were in his time yielded to the mathematical possibility that we were in the past—right back in the past. Included in that was the motion of the planet, since a miscalculation would have resolved us in empty space due to this world having traveled in its orbit. What we have to do is reverse the factors he used. Since all action is mental, that is our only course. The physical will automatically follow."

"Well, we can try," the Amazon said, without much conviction. To her things were essentially material, and venturing into the metaphysical realms of Abna was something new, though she was aware from previous experiences that, under stress, Abna could achieve the apparently impossible.

"All right," Abna said. "Now—concentrate. Eliminate this from thought. Believe only the other. In time the situation will yield."

He closed his eyes and the others did the same. For Abna the results were rapid because of his mastery of the force of mind over matter. It took him a matter of three minutes to convince himself that the existence he was at present experiencing was nothing more than a probability, and therefore did not really exist—but for the Amazon, Viona, and Mexone the effort was harder to realize.

Little by little the Amazon felt herself slowly mastering the situation. There were vague glimpses of a time—entirely different from the one spawning giant-sized bacteria and atomic fire—glimpses of a placid age in which there seemed to be a quiet and ordered civilization. Then again the vision would fade, and yet again she struggled for it—until finally, with a sudden conscious effort, she broke the probability belief. It no longer represented a fact to her. Instead, the new state of environment was the only one that had meaning.

"It succeeded," she said quietly, looking at Abna. "Now I am perfectly sure that mind can control matter."

"It has always has." Abna looked at her seriously. "It depends if you have the kind of mind which can do it.

You have—but I am wondering if Viona and Mexone will be strong enough."

The Amazon became silent, looking about her. She and Abna appeared to be in some kind of open field. Overhead was a brilliantly burning sun. In the far distance loomed a vague purple suggestion of some kind of city.

"Wondering where we are?" Abna questioned, and as the Amazon slowly nodded he went on, "Back in the time from which Salzner sent us. We've moved a little in space, hence we're not in the actual city itself but some distance from it, and on the surface of the planet. We'll explore that city later—when the others come."

"Things seem extra quiet here, Abna," she commented, surveying the sky and the landscape. "No birds—no animals—no people. One would have thought...."

"Far as I know, it is an empty world," he replied gravely. "Why do you suppose we set to work to destroy the foundations of life back in Time? Now you see the result—far in the future. This planet should be absolutely deserted."

"Then why is it the city of machines is still there—?" The Amazon paused, her brows knitted. "No, it must be some other kind of city. The machines were underground: there wasn't anything above surface. Abna!" She turned on him in sudden alarm. "Something's gone wrong somewhere. That looks like a city in the distance—yet formerly the whole planet was deserted on the surface."

"There is no guarantee that we landed back in exactly the right place," he answered. "We shall have to—"

He paused, his unspoken sentence forgotten, as something merged out of the air close by. It wavered for a second, disappeared, then came back into full strength. It was Viona....

"Dad!" she cried thankfully, hurrying forward. "And Mother! We made it then— Or at least I did so. She glanced around anxiously. "I thought Mexone would be—"

She did not need to finish her sentence. In a matter of seconds Mexone had accomplished the feat also, and came from dim transparency to solid flesh and blood. He stood for a moment, smiling at his own achievement.

"Well, that's that difficulty overcome," Abna said, as Mexone came forward. "We've pulled ourselves out of a past time into a future one, and as near as possible we tried to envisage the time from which we came—when Sazner was in control. Now I begin to wonder—not about the destruction of Sazner and his race, since that was inevitable with the ancestral props destroyed—but exactly where we've come. As your Mother pointed out, Viona, that city in the distance has no right to be there. When we left, everything was underground."

"There is another point too," Mexone observed. "When we were in the other plane of time, it was night: here it is day."

Abna did not comment. He was looking at his shadow. In fact he studied it for several minutes, never taking his eyes off it—then at last he looked up in vague astonishment.

"The sun," he said, "isn't moving. Or rather the planet is not. It has no revolution."

The Amazon stared at him. "But—but that's impossible!"

"Not really. Take the example of our own Earth—so very far away. When eventually it nears the end of its life, it will stand with one face to the sun, the original spin gone, and the brake of tidal action finally slowing it to a standstill. The same thing must have happened here."

"In which case there's no *Ultra*," Viona said. "If by some mischance we've come to another world, what are we to do? Is it possible, father, that we have so altered things that we have come to a different planet entirely?"

"That doesn't seem possible." Abna was staring into the distance in complete perplexity. Finally he made up his mind. "There is no use in us standing here conjecturing. We've got to find out what has gone wrong. The best thing we can do is head for that city on the horizon. Come on...."

CHAPTER NINE
1,000-YEAR ERROR

All of them noticed as they progressed how changed this world was from the one of Sazner. It had land that was perfectly arable, gentle breezes, and everlasting sunshine. Nothing further from the thin-aired underground planet possessed by Sazncr and his race could possibly be imagined.... And the city too was entirely different. It was more Earthly than anything yet, and not composed of the cone-like edifices which had formerly been so predominant.

The main entrance to the city appeared to be by a single road, which ran out into the wilderness and then just stopped. It was composed of a material that had no earthly parallel. Not that the four were particularly interested: their eyes were fixed ahead on the busy life of this mysterious metropolis. That it was populated was more than obvious. There were vehicles moving in the street; fast aircraft flying through the upper heights and pedestrians by the thousands—if pedestrians they were. They had about them something of the urgency of workers as they went about their various tasks.

"Do you notice something?" the Amazon asked

abruptly. "Not one of these tulip people is scarlet."

It was a surprising fact, but nonetheless true. Every one of Sazner's race had been of the same hue as himself—and yet here were all colors except red.

"It begins to look as though we're on the right tack after all," Abna said. "Sazner's race has evidently disappeared and given place to these new tulip people...."

Immediately there was a disturbance, a gathering of tulip-shaped bodies and a blank faceless stare in the quartet's direction—then a few of them ventured forward.

"Think they're dangerous?" the Amazon asked tautly.

"No. In any case we've no weapons to do anything about it. Just have to take what comes."

What did come proved to be a jabber of strange language, much the same as the quartet had experienced upon their first arrival on Vashon's planet. Then, seeing that their conversation did no good, one of them resorted to his telepathic powers. Immediately, what seemed to be a voice became apparent to the four at one and the same time.

"Who are you? What are you doing here?"

"Time travelers," Abna answered, at a loss for anything else to say. "We are unarmed and would have audience with your ruler. Perhaps you can aid us?"

"Follow me," ordered the tulip-being, who seemed to have appointed himself the leader.

"Doesn't seem to be any sign of danger," the Amazon commented, as they mounted the steps. "In fact, I don't think I ever saw such co-operative people. But all the time at the back of my mind is the one insistent question— Who are they? Why are they so different from Sazner and his people?"

They had entered a long, broad hall and were following their solitary escort before Abna spoke.

"Seems to be entirely different race altogether. There must be an answer...."

He did not attempt any further suggestions there and then. He was content to wait and see—and at length their journey through the lofty halls ended in a room of wide proportions and tasteful furnishings, even though everything was of the same odd, unearthly pattern. Apparently the individual already present had been informed by some mysterious process of his visitors' arrival, for he did not appear the least surprised to see them. He was already waiting.

"My greetings to you, my friends." His telepathic communication came immediately. "I understand you are time travelers."

"Well—er—yes," Abna said, somewhat surprised.

The being made a motion with his tentacle, at which the escort turned and departed. In the brief pause that ensued the four were conscious of an intense mental appraisement.

"I am not the ruler," the tulip-being 'said' suddenly. "I am merely acting for him. When Jix—the individual who brought you here—informed me by telepathy of your coming, I made the necessary preparations to receive you. My name is Risa, and I am chief adviser to the ruler, of which there is one for this entire planet. We are no longer split into groups, as was the case in Vashon's day. Not that you will know of him."

"Vashon!" The Amazon gave a start. "Are you then members of his race? From the neighbor world to this?"

"Certainly we are. This planet has been colonized by our home world."

"It is because of Vashon that we are here—" the Amazon hesitated. "That is—partly. The real reason for our being here is to find the *Ultra*, our space machine, so that we can depart into the void."

There was puzzlement in Risa's thoughts. Then he formed them into intelligible communication.

"Can it be...." He stopped, plain astonished. "Can it be that you are the four who saved our home planet? Or at least the race upon it, Vashon's race, of so long ago?"

"So—long ago?" Abna repeated.

"I must explain," the adviser hurried on. "Our home world, so I understand from the history records, was under the menace of Sazner, an alien scientist from this world who desired to age the planet for his own radio-active race. He all but succeeded, when an amazing thing happened. His entire race disappeared from this world—and not only that, but a multitude of machines over which he and his fellow scientists had control. It appeared that in some way they had control of the atom and its relation to Time and Space. Then suddenly— nothing! Overnight, as you might say. There was no explanation. But there was a report in the history records concerning four travelers from a distant planet who were waging a crusade against Sazner.... Can it be that by some miracle you are those four?"

"We are," the Amazon said grimly; then she glanced at Abna, "Apparently your plan worked, Abna."

"So it would appear...." And he added a detailed explanation for Risa's benefit. For quite a time it appeared as though the adviser was struggling to understand. His thoughts were completely confused—then out of his bewilderment emerged a question.

"Am I to understand that through the destruction of amoeba in a past time you destroyed Sazner's race?"

"Exactly so," the Amazon continued. "Since it appeared that Sazner and his race were limited to one planet—this one—it seemed logical to my husband that the destruction of the amoeba, the primordial ancestors of the race—would stop the race from ever evolving. All life is an illusion. It only exists because we believe it. We destroyed the belief. Or, in scientific terms, we eliminated the possibility that Sazner and race, as aggregates of atoms, had ever been."

"Yes—I understand." It was perfectly clear that the adviser did nothing of the sort, but he had to save his face. "Which would account for the machinery disappearing as well. It simply did not exist, any more than did Sazner and his race. But there is one other factor which you have perhaps not taken into account."

"Such as?" Abna asked quickly.

"The matter of your spaceship which you say you have come to retrieve. That presumably went too."

Abna reflected swiftly. "I suppose, he mused, "that

everything belonging to the race would be involved in the time alteration. When their underground city of machines disappeared, the *Ultra* would have been isolated underground...."

"And," the Amazon interposed, "when the underground strata reformed about it, it would have been caught up in a tremendous explosion. No two objects can occupy the same space at the same time. That is something we never bargained for!"

"Yet the fact remains," the adviser 'said.' "When our home planet was found to be no longer in danger, we examined the world of Sazner to see what had happened. Or rather my ancestors did. I am speaking purely from my knowledge of history. It was discovered that it was an empty planet, and as such useful for taking the rapidly growing population. We were fast becoming overcrowded, and so my race annexed this world. But even into this entered a new element of danger...."

"Oh?" the Amazon asked, rather vaguely, for she was trying to imagine what was to be done now the *Ultra* was gone.

"We found that the sun was dying, and that of course involved all the planets. Finally, the scientists evolved a plan whereby the sun could be regenerated, and at the same time our surplus population could be transferred here."

Abna frowned. "But I thought the race belonging to Vashon had no advanced scientific knowledge? They left all that to Sazner.... How long ago was this?"

"Oh...." Hesitation. "Roughly 1,000 of your years—as I read from your mind how you calculate time. At any rate, I am speaking of a time long ago."

The Amazon gasped. "Do—you mean to say that we miscalculated our return by 1,000 years? That all this happened 1,000 years ago?"

"It did," the adviser conceded, his thoughts grave.

The four looked at each other in dismay. An error had been possible in their own calculations, of course, a slight error of a few years this way or that, but 1,000 years...!

"You learned then to navigate space?" Abna inquired, at last.

"Yes. But one must have the motive power with which to travel, and everything has been fired into the sun. Our stock of copper from all the planets is at zero. We can survive maybe 100 of your years. Certainly no longer."

The Amazon moved restlessly. "It appears that in having saved Vashon's world from destruction so long ago, we have only produced a temporary relief. Now every world is faced with disaster, this time from natural causes."

"I am sure we are most grateful to you," Risa said. "I am delighted that it has fallen to my lot to thank the four who saved the people of Vashon. But for your intervention the race would certainly have perished and Sazner would have taken over a radioactive world as he intended.... The one great disaster, from your point of view, is the loss of your space machine. If only we had enough fuel for one of our own machines—"

"No, no." The Amazon shook her head quickly. "Your vessels would never be capable of making the journeys which are commonplace to us. Scores of light years at one flight.... It is out of the question. And anyway, you have no copper fuel." She turned and looked at Abna. "Any suggestions, Abna? Our work is not done yet by any means. We set out to save these people, and to a certain extent we managed it. Now we face a second trouble."

"It requires thought," Abna replied slowly, meditating. "Our own predicament can wait for the moment. We can stay here as well as anywhere else.... Risa, do I understand that you have replenished your dying sun by firing copper into it, the intra-atomic energy of which has temporarily restored it?"

"That is so. If you wish, I can show you the full scientific process involved; then perhaps you may be able to arrive at some conclusion."

Abna nodded. "It would be as well. In the meantime, the four of us will stay here as guests and occupy our time in an endeavor to find a solution. Is that agreeable?"

"Quite," the adviser responded promptly. "I will acquaint the ruler with your decision, and I will also inform our scientists of your arrival. Among you— though I doubt it—you may find an answer to our problem."

CHAPTER TEN
THE COPPER PLANET

Had circumstances been normal, the quartet could have enjoyed the facilities that were offered them. They had every comfort, they were the guests of the highest in the land, and they also had the opportunity to understand these quiet, flower-like beings more intimately. But back of their minds was the constant nagging worry of the loss of the *Ultra*, and in a different sense their self-inflicted task of saving the sun of this remote system in the Milky Way. Normally, perhaps, they would not have preoccupied themselves with this task, but they were convinced that here was a genuine, peaceable people striving to make the most of their scientific achievements—now Sazner was eliminated—and yet stalked by a malignant fate that would reach its zenith within 100 years.

"The facts," Abna said, "are now quite clear. Thanks to the co-operation of the scientists, we know what they did to gain a temporary life from their sun...."

He was speaking on the third 'day' of their stay—day in so far that night was unknown on this side of the planet. Listening to him, ready to offer any helpful suggestion, were the Amazon, Viona, and Mexone, disported in various parts of the great room that had been placed at their disposal for living purposes.

"Apparently," Abna continued, studying the charts, "the scientists have made tremendous strides in the 1,000 years which have passed. They have succeeded in making each planet habitable, even that world of monsters upon which Sazner tried to crash us. But in regard to this particular planet, they have accomplished a very fine piece of engineering. First they have slowed down the revolution to zero by tilting the axis, so that the energy of the sun is concentrated on one spot and is not diffused over both sides of the planet. Apparently only the sunlit side is populated. Second, they have given the sun fresh energy by extracting from each planet the maximum of copper, firing it into the sun at regular intervals by automatic means. This is the situation now.... The copper has run out. The present level of energy in the sun may exist for 100 years, then will come the collapse of the sun and its natural reversion to a nova. That—is the end."

The Amazon glanced at him urgently. "Surely there must be some source of copper? All these worlds circling around and not one scrap of copper seems—"

"You forget one thing, mother," Viona remarked. "Even supposing we could locate one, what good would it do us? We've no way of getting there. No *Ultra*, and apparently what space ships there are here are grounded for lack of fuel."

"We'll worry over that when we have to," the

Amazon retorted obstinately. "We've got to sort out this problem somehow.... The sooner we spend a bit of time in the observatory, the better. Agreed, Abna?"

"All right," he shrugged. "It's quite a trip, but maybe it will be worth it."

The journey of which he had spoken was certainly a long one, since it involved traveling from the dayside to the night side of the planet. Here, in a barren wilderness, eternally facing the stars, the flower people maintained an observatory. Abna had only to make his wishes be known and within half an hour the quartet was on its way by fast plane, flying high over the populated regions, eventually through a band of ever darkening twilight, and ultimately to the night side.

They went swiftly through the lower regions, and up into the observatory tower. Here the normal staff promptly relinquished their various tasks and left the four to themselves.

Abna pressed the button that opened the upper dome to its widest extent, and then stood looking at the cloudless, unfamiliar sky. So different from the view on Earth, with its near view of the Milky Way and the sprawling misty mass of multimillions of stars.

"What are you looking for?" the Amazon asked at last, her violet eyes on the inconceivable immensity of it all.

"A copper-bearing sun, which should be bright green. It is logical to assume that a sun like that will have planets that contain copper in large quantities.... But there are so many stars, so many island universes.

See if you can spot anything."

Viona and Mexone also stepped up to the main balcony and intently studied the incredible heavens. There seemed to be stars of all variety and magnitude—

Then Mexone suddenly gave a cry and pointed steadily.

"There! That's an emerald green color—about the only one there is. In my section of the sky anyhow."

Abna led the way back into the observatory and to focus the spectroscope-reflector on the distant star was but the work of a few moments. Immediately the bright green light appeared on the screen it shifted position until it fell into the grade already computed for it.

"Copper!" Abna exclaimed in delight. "Hardly even a dilution of anything else. A sun composed almost entirely of copper in the gaseous state. Let's hope it has planets. Some suns are quite sterile."

First the sun itself loomed up, an intense blinding green. Immediately Abna cut it out and instead explored the dark wastes in the immediate vicinity of the sun, hunting assiduously for planets. But, at the end of an hour of searching, he had failed to discover any planetary body.

"Smallest solar family on record," Abna commented sourly. "Not even one solitary planet!"

"Don't be so hasty, Abna," the Amazon said, studying the readings, and sliding into the seat vacated by Abna. "That green star is actually only a couple of light-years distant from here. It's the nearest star to this solar system—and exceptionally so."

"So what?" Abna said. "It doesn't have any planets—"

"Not *now* it doesn't," the Amazon interrupted impatiently. "But doesn't that suggest possibilities to you?"

As Abna gave a shrug, Viona broke in excitedly: "I think I get your meaning, Mother! The two systems are so close together, astronomically speaking, that maybe some time in the past, the green star *did* have a planet, one on the very rim of that solar system—like Pluto in our own solar system. Only for—"

"—only for something to have happened that knocked it out of its orbit," the Amazon finished. "If such a cosmic accident had happened, that planet might very well have drifted towards the gravitational well of *this* system...."

"But Risa's scientists have already told us they've already travelled to each planet in this system, and have denuded them of copper," Mexone objected, frowning.

The Amazon flashed him an impatient glance as she made adjustments to the giant reflector. "Yes, but they probably never looked or travelled any great distance beyond the orbit of their known outermost planet. They only have conventional space ships, remember. Ah! I think I have something—"

The others crowded around her as she pointed to the displayed image of interstellar space, completely black, except for patches of distant glowing nebulae and pinpricks of light denoting the nearer stars.

"See that?" the Amazon murmured. "In the top right-hand corner? There's a tiny circular patch of black against that background nebula...."

Thereafter the Amazon recalibrated the giant telescope, and the Crusaders used every resource in the observatory to bring the distant black occlusion into closer focus. After another two hours they had proved the Amazon's theory to the hilt: it *was* a planet, lying well beyond the orbit of the outermost of the known planets, a cosmic wanderer that had drifted into the interstellar gulf between Risa's system and its parent green star, to pursue a lonely elliptical orbit between the two suns.

"Right now it's some four billion miles from us," the Amazon announced. "No air, of course; after its plunge through interstellar space it'll be completely frozen to its surface. Any life it might have once had has been obliterated. Size about the same as Earth, but with a greater gravity.... But the essential thing is that the planet is positively weighted down with copper. There's enough there and to spare."

Abna stopped the motors on the telescope and restored the lighting to normal, then he stood thinking.

"Now we come to the problem," he said at length. "Four billion miles away is a world about the size of Earth containing all the copper that is necessary. Enough to keep the sun of this system going for as long as the race exists. Enough to power the space machines; enough to power a new *Ultra* if we can rebuild.... But how do we cross the gulf, and even more important, how do we bring the copper back?"

Silence. Each one was wrestling with the problem,

and there appeared to be no solution.

"Is it possible," Mexone asked, who had been doing some hard thinking on his own account, "to bring the entire planet within reach of us?"

Abna and the Amazon looked at him in surprise for a moment. It was one of those statements, which, though uttered by one who had not nearly the experience of the elder people, had withal a grain of possibility.

Abna stood lost in thought for a moment. "To bring a planet the size of Earth across four billion miles of space will take all the resources this world possesses— And I am none too sure that we will be successful, either. We might start it advancing towards us, but imagine the disaster if we failed to stop it. It would smash this world in pieces and upset the whole system."

"Naturally," the Amazon said, her scientific enthusiasm fully fired, "we shall have to work out everything in detail. It's the only way, Abna—and credit to Mexone for thinking of it."

The four were silent again, moving restlessly around the observatory as they tried to give birth to the right idea. At length it was Mexone who spoke again.

"Would it make any difference if that world of copper were smashed in pieces?"

Abna glanced at him. "Not the slightest. The mass would still be there, even though the bulk was broken up."

"But what if it is spread out evenly? I mean like a sea on both sides of this world. There would be disturbances, no doubt, but nothing serious. There would not be as much upset as a solid single body."

"Like—like the rings of Saturn," Viona put in brightly. "As anybody knows, they're not really rings, but millions of small bodies and—"

"Mexone has another good idea there," the Amazon interrupted. "Look, Abna, I think the best thing to do is contact the chief scientists of this planet and tell them what we have in mind. We are planning all sorts of things without knowing what resources we possess."

So a move was made to the lower quarters of the observatory where all the executive work was done. It was not long before the head astronomer had contacted the leading scientists, and within a short time the strange, flower-like beings were hastening to Abna's plans. When he had finished there was a meditative pause, then came the leading scientist's thought-waves.

"You are to be congratulated, my friends, on locating a copper-bearing planet. We never suspected its existence, so far out from our known system. As to the rest of your plan, there seems to be nothing impossible about it except one thing. We have no means whereby to smash this distant planet up."

"You haven't such a thing as force projector?" the Amazon asked.

"No. I'm afraid not. Such a device is not yet within the reach of our knowledge.... But perhaps you have some other idea of your own?"

"Quite a few," Abna responded. "Somehow, that planet has got to be broken up into pieces. After that the parts must all be de-gravitated and—"

"De-gravitated?" the scientist interrupted, puzzled.

Abna gave the Amazon a glance. "Rendered incapable of being drawn into that planet's sun," Abna elaborated. "That is essential. The natural consequence of blowing the planet to pieces will be for the pieces to fall into its nearest field of attraction. That we have to counterbalance."

"It is a system entirely beyond us," the scientist confessed. "We shall have to leave it to you. How do you propose to move the pieces of this planet across space? Since during that time they will not be subject to gravitation, how can you have any effect on them?"

"You are confusing gravitation with magnetism," Abna replied. "The two things are totally different. A de-gravitated object is not subject to the attraction of other bodies in its vicinity, but it is subject to magnetism. From this planet we will reach out with a magnetic attraction to pull the pieces towards us. We will continue to do that until they have passed the borderline of gravitations between the two suns—all of which has to be worked out to the last detail, of course—and by that time the de-gravitational effect will have gone off. The only remaining point is how to smash that planet into pieces when you have no such thing as a force projector."

"Use a sufficiently powerful atomic bomb and the thing is done," Viona said, spreading her hands.

"Quite so," the Amazon conceded, "but how do we get the bomb there? Again, how do we de-gravitate the pieces without being close to the planet? As you know, it is only a matter of a minute or so to create de-gravitation, but one has to be on the spot. With no space machine to—"

"How far did you say?" interrupted the scientist's thoughts. "Was it four billion miles?"

Abna nodded, at which the scientist rose and went over to a communicator. He was engaged for some time talking in his weird flute-like language to an unknown: then he came back to the table.

"We have just enough copper left in our last reserves for one space machine to make a journey of that length—but not back," he announced. "Most of the journey out would involve simply coasting, having built up speed, and would not require the expenditure of fuel beyond that needed to build up to maximum velocity. The machine is small, but at least it will do the trip. But don't forget we need keep a smaller reserve for a second ship here to pick up supplies of copper from nearby space, once it comes within range—" he broke off, frowning at another disturbing thought. "But the distance is so colossal, that it would take several years to complete the outward journey!"

"It wouldn't take us anything like so long!" Viona interrupted. "To *your* people, perhaps, but *our* physical constitutions are such that we can easily withstand swift and constant acceleration, building up to almost the speed of light, if need be. That way the journey can be made in about a week. I suppose we'd use a lot of the fuel in deceleration too, in order to slow down and orbit the planet when we reach it...but we only need the copper to carry us one way," Viona added, brightening. "Once we reach the planet we have all the copper we need."

"It begins to take form," the Amazon declared, her eyes brightening. "We will go to this world, Abna, and—"

"That cannot be," he replied quietly. "Both of us will need to be here to control the magnetism to draw the pieces towards us. These scientists here have no knowledge of the system used, so we'll have to do it ourselves. There must be no chance of a mistake. No, I'm afraid the task of dropping the atom bomb and producing the de-gravitation falls to Viona and Mexone."

Mexone rubbed his hands. "About time we had a chance to do something! I've no objections— What about you, Viona?"

"Lead me to it," she smiled.

"Then the preliminary details are solved," Abna said. "Now comes the job of working out everything mathematically, so there can be no mistake. And you, my friends," he glanced at the scientists, "will have to help us."

* * * * * * *

The first thing to be completed was the nuclear bomb. In size it was no larger than a pineapple, but its potential power was stupendous.

"I wish,'" Abna said thoughtfully, studying the bomb as it stood in its rack on the laboratory bench, "that I could foresee the entire outcome of this explosion."

The Amazon glanced in surprise. "The outcome? But surely we've worked it all out?"

"As far as is possible, yes—stresses and strains and explosive quality, but apart from the normal elements of a nuclear bomb, we have certain materials which are peculiar to this world. Radioactive stuff. We've never had the chance to find out how they will react when their inner power is released."

The Amazon thought for a moment, and then shrugged. "There just are not enough materials left to make a test. Everything has been packed into the bomb itself.... Needless worry, Abna, I'm sure."

Finally, the magnetizer was completed. This had been a matter of engineering at a chosen site—a lonely spot on the night side of the planet. Immediately the news came through, the quartet wasted no time in going with the scientists to view this last link in the campaign—and a very impressive sight it was too.

"Well," Abna said, after a return to the observatory had been made, "there remains nothing but to brief you, Viona and Mexone, in what you have to do. You have been instructed already as to how to handle the space machine, and these are the rest of your orders...."

Mexone and Viona listened intently, never once interrupting.

"You will approach to within 500,000 miles of the copper planet, and will then release the bomb. You are aiming at no particular target, so accuracy doesn't enter into it. It will inevitably hit the planet because it is the one source of attraction. The planet will disintegrate—at least we hope so—but dissipation of the pieces will not be immediate because of the forces of cohesion in empty space. You will have something that resembles a cracked nut, with the pieces drifting further and further away from each other. The moment you have accomplished this, you will notify us by radio. By the time your signal reaches us, the initial disturbance will almost have subsided. The moment it does so, you will switch on the de-gravitator. Meanwhile, immediately we get your radio signal, we will get to work with the magnetic attractor. Even traveling at the speed of light, the magnetic beam will not reach you across four billion miles immediately. That delay will give you time to grab yourselves a chunk of copper to use as fuel on your return journey, before retreating a safe distance from the asteroidal field. That way our actions will be coordinated, and we will overcome and actually make use of the time lag between us. That will mean that the pieces of the planet will be drawn this way without any counter gravitational pull from the copper planet's sun.... After that it is our own worry to so dispose the pieces that they fall into place in a widely scattered field. By that time the de-gravitational effect will have worn off and we shall be able to use a counterbalance between the two suns. That, however, is not your concern. You have your individual orders.... Any questions?"

"Only one," Viona said, "When we have done our job and refuelled, do we come straight back, or do we wait until you have got the pieces sorted out to your liking?"

"Delay your return until you get a radio signal from us, otherwise you will be caught in the field of the magnetic attractor beam and that may cause trouble.... Right?"

"Check," Viona agreed promptly. "When do we start?"

"In half an hour. You'd better get along to your space machine. Your mother and I will be remaining here to direct operations."

Viona nodded. She gave the signal to Mexone, and together they went on their way to the pre-chosen spot where the space machine was waiting. The fact that they were to carry a bomb of overwhelming force seemed to be the last thing that concerned them.

"I wish," Abna said thoughtfully, "I could rid myself of an uneasy premonition regarding those two...." He shrugged. "Well, nothing we can do about it. We have our own part of the plan to work out. Better stand by the radio for Viona's messages. It will be some considerable time before they can reach the planet."

Meanwhile, Viona and Mexone had reached the small machine, which had been equipped as far as possible to suit their requirements. The bomb itself was strapped into a special matrix under the belly of the ship, a completely foolproof device invented by Abna. Nothing could dislodge the bomb until a switch was operated from within the vessel.

"All set," Viona commented, as she made a final check-over in the company of three of the flower-like ground staff. "Bomb fixed and de-gravitator in posítion...."

Finally Viona was satisfied. She dismissed the ground crew and closed the airlock; then she glanced across at Mexone as he stood beside the radio equipment.

"Start telling them we're departing," she instructed, settling before the control board. "After that merely give reports as we get further and further away.... Ready?"

"Ready!" Mexone confirmed, and raised the microphone. Thereafter his voice intoned steadily as the little machine lifted and climbed with ever increasing speed into the void. Viona smiled, enjoying the sensation of being captain of the ship, but she could not help but notice how inefficient the vessel was compared to the mighty *Ultra*. However, it was serving its purpose and that was all that signified.

In a matter of minutes the world below was commencing to assume the contour of a planetary globe. In fifteen minutes it was a slowly receding world in the void and, far ahead, and invisible as yet, was the solitary planet that was their destination.

CHAPTER ELEVEN
INTO THE UNKNOWN

The journey to the copper planet was more or less uneventful, as far as alarms were concerned. Viona and Mexone, both superhumanly strong, were equal to the crushing constant acceleration necessary to build up speed and reduce the journey time. Every now and again they sent back radio communication. It took the same form each time, giving the distance and reporting no untoward incidents. The further they traveled, the longer became the gaps between radio messages being transmitted and received. Minutes gradually extended into hours...then at last the four billion mile gap had narrowed tremendously and the copper world was filling all the void in front of them. It was the time to stir to vital action.

"It's a dead world all right," Viona said, peering down upon it, and relaying her voice over the radio. "Nothing but rock from the looks of it—but that rock is, of course, copper covered by a deep layer of meteoric dust and frozen atmosphere. Altogether a highly inhospitable spot."

"Our instructions are to orbit at 500,000 miles and

release the bomb," Mexone said.

Viona nodded, and turned back to the radio. "I shall not report until the bomb is gone and has exploded according to plan. Present communication ends."

She switched off and settled herself intently in the control seat. "Be several hours before Mother and father receive that radio message, of course, but it doesn't signify. Everything has already been worked out in advance."

Mexone, beside her, put his hand on the bomb release switch and waited. There were moments of growing intensity, with the distance indicator swinging slowly, and lessening the miles.

"Stand by," Viona muttered at length. "We're about at the point now."

The girl reopened the radio link, took one last survey of the indicators, then looked at Mexone and gave a nod. Instantly he depressed the release switch.

"Bomb gone!" Viona said briefly, and instantly swung the vessel into an orbit at a distance of 500,000 miles. They needed to be at what had been adjudged a safe distance when the bomb exploded—yet just the same, the unholy fascination of watching it explode could not be denied.

"Here!" Mexome said swiftly, and slipped a pair of deep purple goggles over her eyes, then he did the same for himself.

As far as Viona was concerned, she was incapable of seeing anything anymore. She was flying the machine blind, but the safe orbit had already been established, and she was secure in the knowledge that she could not possibly collide with anything.... The time that elapsed between the bomb being released and it coming to the end of its half million miles fall seemed endless. Had there been any atmosphere worth mentioning, the bomb would undoubtedly have exploded with the friction. Since there was not, it kept on dropping with ever increasing swiftness, completely invisible.

"How much longer?" Viona breathed. "Maybc it's a dud, hasn't gone off or something—"

She stared back through the rear observation port. She could only just make out details through the purple polarized glass. Mexone came and stood at her side, his unconsciously strong grip on her shoulder positively hurting—

Then, suddenly, the bomb exploded.

Even through the purple glasses the flash was so intolerable that it stung the eyes. It paled the remote sun into insignificance, and the stars were swallowed up in the effulgence. Naturally it was only brief, then darkness complete appeared to drop down. There was an aching pause, then shock waves, carried on the melted atmosphere of the formerly frozen exploded planet as they began to spread out through the void.

"That certainly was some mixture dad used," Viona breathed. "Shocks are still coming— In fact," she added, with an edge of alarm in her voice, "they're getting stronger than before. How can that be—"

She could not speak any further as the machine rocked and pivoted before the most violent shock of all. There was something strange here. By all normal processes the explosion should have quickly spent itself in a radioactive cloud, but instead of that the haze over the doomed planet was deepening and for some reason turning into a pale lilac color. At the same time impact after impact came shattering through the void.

"I don't like this!" Viona's voice held fear. "Something queer—"

"We've got to stick around though to put on the de-gravitator," Mexone interrupted urgently. "Maybe we'd better put it on now before anything happens."

Mexone dived for the equipment, but before he could start up the power and release the switch his attention was caught by something from the shattered world below. The lilac color had taken on a mysterious form and was shafting into space in a titanic bar. Such it appeared to be, at least, and in a matter of seconds it hit the tiny space machine as it circled desperately.

"Mexone—!" Viona screamed.

He dashed across to aid her, and at that identical moment the lavender beam struck the ship. What happened then neither Viona nor Mexone had the least idea.... They had a brief sense of overwhelming shock, of being torn apart and put together again in a fraction of a second. Lights danced in front of them and there was an unspeakable sickness weighing them down.

Then calm. They moved slowly, traces of pain slowly vanishing. From their position on the floor they got gradually to their knees and crawled to the outlook port, expecting to see that shattered world below and the lavender beam extinguished. Instead they saw the unbelievable— A mighty purple haze covered the infinite, in which strange forms of incredible giantism lived and moved. It was like a picture of shadows incredibly magnified, illumined with the color of lilac.... And the void and stars had gone.

"Where—where are we?" Viona whispered, stunned.

"Don't know." Mexone's lips quivered. "Some kind of other space.... I'll try to send a radio message to your parents."

He blundered across to it and spoke urgently.

"I don't know if they'll ever receive that," he whispered. "And—and look at the rear port."

Viona turned and gazed with him, stupefied. They could still see people moving, so huge that it was beyond imagination to absorb them. They seemed to have arms and legs and vaguely human outline, but as to the rest it was blurred, unreal, fantastic....

* * * * * * *

Back on the planet that Viona and Mexone had left, Abna and the Amazon were trying to figure things out. The last radio message they had received had reported the release of the bomb. Following that, after an interval whilst the light traveled from beyond the rim of the solar system, they had seen the bewildering flash far out in the heavens.

Then nothing. The darkness of the heavens was back to normal again. Intently the Amazon and Abna studied the telescopic screen. Formerly it had held a view of that distant world; now it showed a monstrous haze of dust and fragments with slowly dispersing gas clouds.

"They've done it, all right," Abna said, a queer note in his voice. "But why didn't they radio immediately following the explosion...or since? Been plenty of time for further messages to have reached us."

The Amazon did not wait to answer the question. She was already at the radio controls, speaking urgently.

"Hello, Viona! Hello, Mexone! Are you receiving me? If you are, report at once. Over."

"Now we have to wait several hours for a reply—unless Viona has already sent a message to us in the interim," the Amazon said tautly. "The situation is intolerable!"

As the radio remained dead, Abna turned sharply from the telescopic screen.

"They're not de-gravitating those parts and pieces either," he said quickly. "Something's wrong! Unless we're careful, all those fragments are going to drift just anywhere and we'll lose the copper."

He watched a second or two longer. The Amazon, her face strained with worry, came over and joined him. For once her scientific interest was drowned by her anxiety for Viona.

"We might just manage it, de-gravitation or otherwise," Abna said urgently, as he fled for the door. "Come on...."

According to plan, a number of the flower people were standing around in the darkness outside ready for immediate emergency action, and they had with them one of their fast ground vehicles. They alerted as the Amazon and Abna appeared, conscious immediately that something was wrong.

"The magnetizer tower, as quickly as possible," Abna shouted, hurrying across to the vehicle, and such was the force of his thoughts the telepaths understood immediately.

Jumping into the vehicle, the Amazon immediately beside him, Abna stared up into the sky, but without the telescope it was impossible to observe anything—except the green star that was the copper-bearing sun. Then the vehicle started up, and gathered frantic speed in the darkness as it hurtled in the direction of the magnetizer tower.

In a matter of minutes the monster of latticed metal had loomed into view, the powerhouses at its base brilliantly lighted. Abna leaped from the vehicle before it had come to a standstill and raced across to the main powerhouse.... Fortunately, his foresight had led him to preset all the controls, so as he came hurrying into the midst of the surprised, flower-like engineers he had no explanations to give, and no controls to operate. He simply slid the power lever into its first notch, then the second, and immediately it was safe to do so, the third. Only then did he relax and turn to the Amazon as she stood near him in the bright light.

"Do you think, at that distance and without the fragments being de-gravitated, that we'll have pull enough?" she asked.

"I'm gambling on it, Vi. Nothing else I can do." Abna gave the reading displays a swift scrutiny. "Everything seems to be all right at the moment. The magnetic beam's going out at full intensity. Best thing you can do is go back to the observatory and let me know by radio what's happening. I've only got the instruments to judge from, which is pretty unsatisfying."

"I'll do that...." The Amazon turned and then hesitated. "Abna, about Viona and Mexone. Do you think they are—"

"I don't know." Abna's voice was taut. "We'll have to deal with that later. There's no time now. Off you go!"

Realizing the urgency of the situation the Amazon shrugged and went on her way. The vehicle promptly conveyed her back to the observatory, and from that moment onwards, helped by the scientists, she was constantly sending reports.

There was still one final task to complete, and Abna did it before he gave himself the opportunity to relax. He reported in full to Risa, the Amazon, as usual, accompanying him.

"So far as this planet is concerned, Risa, our task is finished," Abna announced. "In fact, every planet in the system is assured of new life. You can easily devise the necessary means to project a piece of copper into the sun every time it shows signs of waning, and with a whole asteroid field to choose from there is an infinite supply. You have seen the sky from the night side?"

The adviser's strange head nodded, then his thoughts

came clearly.

"I have seen it, and so has the ruler, and all the immediate dignitaries of the planet. You have performed a wonder, Abna of Jupiter, and we are eternally grateful. Copper without end—or at least for as long as our race shall need it."

"Which puts your system in order," Abna smiled. "First we saved a leap-frogging world from destruction at the hands of Sazner, and now we have saved your sun.... For such purpose the Crusaders came into being. But now we face another and to us a more personal problem. We have to find Viona and Mexone, who haven't been seen or heard of since the original bomb explosion which destroyed the copper planet."

"I did not know of that, my friend, and I am deeply sorry to hear it. What do you imagine can have happened to them?"

"Our only course is to fly out there and investigate. The problem of copper for fuel no longer presents itself. Your own scientists are busy right now harvesting the copper fragments in the second ship, and will be arriving back shortly with their first delivery."

"Do you intend to redesign and build your own space machine for the rescue mission?"

"No time for that," the Amazon put in. "It will take weeks to redesign the *Ultra*. We'll use one of your ordinary spaceships. That is why we are here—to ask permission."

"But of course.... Anything you wish is immediately granted, my friends. That is the least we can do for you."

One of the space machines was made quickly ready. Taking off in it, the Amazon and Abna flashed through the upper atmosphere, then through the midst of the 'rings' of the disintegrated copper planet, and so out into the void.

"What reasonable explanation can there be, Vi?" Abna asked seriously, looking through the observation port. "Viona is not a fool; if there was any means of communicating, she would have done so."

"Naturally," the Amazon agreed, then she tightened her lips. "Obviously she can't—and neither can Mexone. You want to know what I really believe? I think that the bomb released forces which we can only guess at, and that Viona and Mexone were caught up in them."

As Abna merely nodded silent agreement the Amazon turned again to the controls and gradually brought the vessel to full power. Even at its maximum velocity it was a slow business, and the Amazon muttered under her breath at the consequent loss of time involved.

"This is going to take ages," she said at last, getting up. "And no automatic pilot, either. Take over for a while whilst I survey outside."

Abna complied and the Amazon moved over to the observation window. As yet the region from which the copper planet had been blasted was still far away. Finally the Amazon turned to the radio and switched on. She did not know why she did it; it was purely an instinct that had to be obeyed. As nothing came through the loudspeaker except a roar of static from the various radiations in the void, Abna looked at her curiously.

"What's the idea?" he asked finally. "Don't expect to get any messages now, do you?"

"No.... But somehow I—" The Amazon shrugged, her eyes moody. "Just a thought that maybe we—"

She stopped, suddenly stooping intently to the speaker. Abna, too, tautened in his seat, straining to hear above the noise of the vessel's power plant. He was almost sure that for a moment he had heard the drift of a sentence—eerie, faraway, like something in another plane of existence.

"It's a voice!" the Amazon cried. "I'll swear it is!"

She made an adjustment of the controls, and abruptly some of the static diminished. For a moment the voice became clear.

"...calling Amazon and Abna. Are you reading me? Viona calling Amazon and Abna. Are you receiving me?"

"Yes, we are receiving you—" the Amazon looked quickly out of the observation window, but the void remained unchanged. "Come in, please. Come in. Over."

For a long time nothing happened. Both the Amazon and Abna waited in tense anxiety, fearing that perhaps they had all they were going to receive—then the voice resumed, still with that curious other-world quality, and as before it started in the middle of a sentence.

"...and don't know where we are. This is Viona

talking. Listen! The explosion changed everything. We are in another kind of space. We can see shadow people, and gigantic figures that loom up and then disappear.... In a sort of void with stars and planets and—"

The communication stopped dead, and all the Amazon's efforts with the controls failed to restore it. Finally she looked at Abna. By now he had recovered from the initial surprise,

"At least she's alive," he said. "And presumably Mexone is as well— Vi, there's something here that we don't understand. Another space altogether, and that bomb explosion was responsible. It may also account for us receiving that fluke transmission somehow, if it perhaps warped space.... I don't understand the why and wherefore, but we've got to get those two youngsters back."

"Yes, but how?" The Amazon came over to him quickly. "We haven't the least idea what happened. We can't penetrate what we don't understand."

"Only one way to sort the thing out—duplicate the happenings. Make another bomb exactly the same as the first, and stop at the same distance from it. If it happened in one instance, it ought to happen again.... This is something we never dreamed of," he went on, musing. "A different space, shadowy people. Sounds intriguing."

Abna did not waste any more time. He swung the vessel round and at maximum velocity it streaked back to the planet from which it had come. Even so it seemed irritatingly slow.

When finally the trip was over, the two wasted no time in putting the matter before Risa, since he seemed to have virtual control over manufacture, politics, and everything else.

"It is a matter of shelving everything else and concentrating on the one task of making a bomb," Abna explained urgently. "Are you prepared to do that? It will mean that your scientists will—for the time being anyway—have to give their whole attention to the one task and—"

"My friends, say no more about it. As I said before, for your saving of our world and race nothing can be too much in return. I will give you an absolutely free hand."

And he did. The moment Abna had again worked out the details and ingredients of the deadly bomb, it was put into manufacture. He and the Amazon flew around to the various factories and laboratories engaged in making the various parts and kept a constant supervision over activity. If the first bomb had been made quickly, the second one was a record. Within ten days it was complete, exactly to the formula of the original one, and clamped within a newly designed matrix in the base of the spaceship the two intended using.

Risa, who had been standing nearby amid a group of his scientific advisers and various associates, raised a tentacle in final salute.

"I assume, my friends, that this is the last we shall see of you—and our good wishes go with you. Your work has embraced many generations, first in the saving of our original world from the scientific machinations of Sazner; and second you have saved us from a dying sun. That we shall not forget, and a welcome always awaits you here if you ever decide to return."

Abna smiled. "We may—we may not. It depends where the forces of the cosmos take us."

With that he turned aside and passed into the vessel's interior. The Amazon followed him after a final leave-taking of the flower people, and then the power plant roared into life. Within a few minutes the vessel was again in the void, its deadly cargo safely pinned underneath.

"What exactly do we do to explode the bomb?" the Amazon asked. "Viona dropped it on the copper planet, which exploded it. We shall have no such solid object."

Abna was silent for a moment, guiding the machine through the waste of copper asteroids. When finally he had cleared them and the open void was ahead, he turned in his seat.

"I've worked it all out, Vi, but I've had little time to tell you. Normally, if we released the bomb, it would simply keep up with the ship and never explode. The answer is an ejector and self-firing mechanism. An ejector will automatically work, flinging the bomb into space far to one side of us. That, added to the velocity of the ship, will put the bomb at a distance of some 2,000 miles from us before it explodes. Not as much as the distance separating Viona and Mexone from the original explosion, but it is the most that can be managed. We will travel to the approximate spot she occupied at the moment of firing and then— Well, see what happens."

Thereafter conversation was at a low ebb. The ship flew on at the maximum velocity of which it was capable and shifts were taken at the controls.

Gradually, pinpointed by their instruments, and drifting clouds of radioactive residual dust and gas, the area of the original explosion came nearer and Abna swung the vessel's nose round until it was following a course approximating that of Viona. Finally, after what seemed an age of waiting, the approximate spot was reached.

"This is about it," the Amazon announced, studying the computations she and Abna had made between them. "From here she released the bomb, and it fell on the copper world at a distance of a half a million miles.... We shan't be so fortunate. We look like being almost on top of the explosion."

"Afraid?" Abna questioned seriously, and the Amazon's violet eyes looked at him intently.

"When have I ever been that? Not afraid—just curious. To be on the threshold of another space is disquieting, to say the least of it.... But it is Viona who matters. I'm ready when you are."

Abna's hand moved to the matrix-ejector switch. He took one final look at the wastes of stars, noting the bright green nearest star that was the copper sun— then he pulled the switch over and counted the seconds on the chronometer. So fast was the bomb hurled into the void it was impossible to follow its flight. There was only waiting—until the seconds had decreased to firing point.

Then, suddenly, the bomb exploded. At the comparatively near distance, the initial flash was something never to be forgotten. It paled the void, the stars, and the copper sun. Abna and the Amazon closed their eyes, protected by dark goggles, but even then they could see a brief and blinding brilliance, which was gone almost immediately. The instant it had done so, they removed their goggles and moved to the window and gazed out on the source of the disturbance.

Creaming, swirling gases positioned the point of explosion. They had just observed it when the first shock waves made themselves felt. The space machine reeled wildly, utterly out of control, and was flung backwards as though before a stupendous wind.

"That strange lavender light!" Abna cried, still not dislodged from his hold on the window frame. "I never saw anything like it before...."

The Amazon stared at it, fascinated. The violet radiance was born from within the very heart of the explosion and came hurtling outwards at stupendous speed. In a fraction of a second it had caught up with the ship, and to the Amazon and Abna came the overwhelming anguish of twisted and repatterned atoms. They groaned under the pain of it and fell helplessly to the floor. Space seemed to turn inside out and the space machine gave a terrific jolt as though it had been fired from a gun. Then, by degrees, the disturbances and the pain began to relax; and, gradually, all became still.

Abna raised himself slowly from the floor and looked about him. The lighting system was still functioning, but the glow of the green copper sun had gone. Instead, outside, everything seemed a grayish black color.

"I think," he whispered, helping up the Amazon, "that we have done it! Soon find out."

Together they crawled to the window and drew themselves up against it. Together they stared outside, their emotions pretty much the same as Viona and Mexone's had been at their own first sight of the exterior.

"Never," Abna breathed, "was there anything like this! How many patterns can Nature still make, and still be inexhaustible?"

The Amazon did not answer. She too was stunned by the wonder of the view. It was beyond anything she had ever pictured.... Everything was still infused with a lilac haze, which slowly cleared.

The suggestion of purple remained, spreading away into infinite distance. It seemed that the ship was both flying in a void, and yet amidst solid things. It was indescribable.

"People!" Abna said suddenly; then with a sudden doubt, "Or are they?"

Perhaps they were. It was impossible to tell. Something huge and shadowy, yet walking on two legs, came and went. There was a suggestion of a body, of inconceivably big proportions—and then a shadow of this figure stretching transiently into the infinite. Here indeed was something that even the knowledge of the

Amazon and Abna could not yet understand.

"Vi," Ahna said solemnly, "we have an entirely new layout here. And no means so far of getting back. So we must go forward, and it promises to be—"

"Look!" the Amazon cried excitedly, interrupting him and pointing. "Viona's ship! There!"

Surprised, Abna gazed steadily. Then he descried it—a tiny gleaming point moving visibly against the stars, and lighted by an unseen source. It took him a few moments to decide that the outlines of the vessel indeed conformed to those of Viona's machine.

"Yes—it's Viona," he breathed, his arm going about the Amazon's shoulders. "That makes all the difference, Vi. All of us are together again, for I suppose Mexone is there also. The four of us, facing the unknown—and a greater unknown than any we have yet encountered."

The Amazon nodded silently, her beautiful face filled both with relief and anticipation.

"This is a crusade indeed," Abna finished at last, turning to the control board. "We've no idea where we are, but at least we still have power over our machine. We'll join Viona and Mexone, and as to the future...."

He ceased speaking with a certain significance. The Amazon was not listening anyway. She was looking at that distant ship amid the stars—stars such as she had never known before, gleaming like diamonds on purple velvet.

Slowly, the space machine changed course....

ABOUT THE AUTHOR

British writer **JOHN RUSSELL FEARN** was born near Manchester, England, in 1908. As a child he devoured the science fiction of Wells and Verne, and was a voracious reader of the Boys' Story Papers. He was also fascinated by the cinema, and first broke into print in 1931 with a series of articles in *Film Weekly*.

He then quickly sold his first novel, *The Intelligence Gigantic*, to the American magazine, *Amazing Stories*. Over the next fifteen years, writing under several pseudonyms, Fearn became one of the most prolific contributors to all of the leading US science fiction pulps, including such legendary publications as *Astounding Stories*, *Startling Stories*, *Thrilling Wonder Stories*, and *Weird Tales*.

During the late 1940s he diversified into writing novels for the UK market, and also created his famous superwoman character, The Golden Amazon, for the prestigious Canadian magazine, the Toronto *Star Weekly*. In the early 1950s in the UK, his fifty-two novels as "Vargo Statten" were bestsellers, most notably his novelization of the film, *Creature from the Black Lagoon*.

Apart from science fiction, he had equal success with westerns, romances, and detective fiction, writing an amazing total of 180 novels—most of them in a period of just ten years—before his early death in 1960. His work has been translated into nine languages, and continues to be reprinted and read worldwide.